We scrimmage the Peewee B's who use the other half of the ice at the same time we practice. The Peewee B's are big. I am the smallest player on our team. They can't resist trying to wipe me out. I can really skate, so they never really hit me with their clumsy goon checks, but it distracts me. Today I score on the first shift, though, a high shot the goalie flinches from. When I'm skating back up ice the goalie nails me in the ankle with the corner of his stick. It catches me just right and I go down with a yelp.

I hear some grunting and yelling, so I look while I lie on the ice and see Woodsie kneeling on the goalie's chest and pounding him in the mask with both gloves.

Before you know it, fights have broken out all over.

## *Other Novels by Bruce Brooks*

# CODY

# BRUCE BROOKS

A LAURA GERINGER BOOK

**HarperTrophy®**
*A Division of HarperCollinsPublishers*

## To Alex

Harper Trophy® is a registered trademark of
HarperCollins Publishers Inc.

Cody
Copyright © 1997 by Bruce Brooks

Library of Congress Cataloging-in-Publication Data
Brooks, Bruce.
    Cody / by Bruce Brooks.
        p.      cm. — (The Wolfbay Wings ; #3)
    "A Laura Geringer book."
    Summary: Eleven-year-old Cody, who plays both hockey and guitar, tries to combine his two interests by forming a fledgling band with some of his teammates, but he is presented with a difficult choice when a conflict develops.
    ISBN 0-06-440599-0 (pbk.)  —  ISBN 0-06-027541-3 (lib. bdg.)
[1. Hockey—Fiction. 2. Musicians—Fiction. 3. Bands (Music)—Fiction.]  I. Title.      II. Series: Brooks, Bruce. Wolfbay Wings ; #3
PZ7.B7913Co      1997                                    97-2052
[Fic]—dc21                                                    CIP
                                                                  AC

Typography by Steve Scott
4    5    6    7    8    9    10
❖
First Edition
Visit us on the World Wide Web!
http://www.harperchildrens.com

J F
BRO

# one

**M**e and Zip got a gig.

One Tuesday night I was over in his basement and we were playing. I had found this cool chord—I was thinking it must almost be a real one, because my left fingers looked so stretched the way left hands played on *Unplugged*. It sounded pretty good too, and all four of my fingers were actually holding the strings down all the way and the two strings left open jangled great against the ones I was pinning down. I was slamming the chord for a while, then Zip said, "Sound it out, man," and slowed his drumming down to a cool slow *boom-boppa-boom* on the floor tom-tom. I slowed down too and did my pick across the strings so you could hear each one separate for a second. It was awesome. Then we speeded up again and I started whanging my pick up fast from the bottom to the top for a change, and that was awesome too.

Then the guy comes in.

He's a high school kid. I see him around sometimes, he lives somewhere around here; he's always alone, and I thought he was kind of weird. He has a nose ring and all the hair cut off one side of his head and never wears a coat but only this big flannel shirt with the elbows out, and he wears these green boots he must have bought at an Army store, they're really *green*. He's always reading some thick book while he walks. My brother, who isn't really a nerd himself, has told me about the sci-fi nerds in high school. They are, like, the worst, and I thought maybe this guy was one. So anyway, this kid isn't legally a stranger, but he does open Zip's basement door and just steps in, which, you know, is sort of unusual.

We stop playing and Zip says, "Who the bleep are you?"

"You guys got something going," he says. "I've heard you before when I walk by some nights."

"So?" I say.

He looks at me. "That was a righteous chord you had there."

I can't help feeling a little good, but I just kind

of grunt and twist at a tuning key.

He looks at Zip. "You change speeds great. Sudden. It's . . . confident."

I'm sure Zip has never exactly used that word to describe his whacking at the drums, but instead of laughing he decides to accept it and he actually says, "Thanks."

Then the guy looks at us both and says, "So, do you want a gig?"

"You mean play for people? Somewhere else?"

The kid laughs. "Unless you can talk your parents into hosting a party for fifty kids in their basement here, yes. It would be at the elementary school. The cafeteria has a stage."

"A *school*?" I say.

He looks at me and nods. Then he has to flip his hair back with his hand, and I can tell it's as automatic for him as putting the puck from backhand to forehand is for me. Which means he's had this haircut a long time, which is kind of cool. Other kids are just starting to do halfhead cuts.

"It's, like, a party, all approved and everything. The high school literary magazine holds one every fall when the first issue gets published. The kids are arty-punk types." He looks a little embarrassed. "They're not dweebs or anything, but they're not exactly headbangers."

"And what will they do while we play?" Zip asks. "Sit around and read?"

"Maybe they get naked and paint each other," I say.

"No, sorry," the kid says with a nice laugh. "Some will just hang around and talk, some will goof around and laugh, and some will stand near the stage and listen. A lot will dance."

"*Dance?*" says Zip.

"To *us*?" I say. "*That* sounds nuts."

The kid laughs again.

"I'm just saying I know some kids who I think will really like your music."

"That's even more nuts."

"Yeah. We, like, don't, you know, think this is like *music* or anything. It's just—I don't know—"

"Sound," the kid suggests.

Something about the way he says it makes Zip suspicious. "Yes," he says, in a phony voice like a guidance counselor uses. "The true, spontaneous, uncontrolled sound of the Young Generation.

Neo-grunge, the spastic hash of the *real* true totally uncrafted universe of preteens. The new, no-chord, free-beat *trash* sound."

Now the guy really laughs. "I can't deny that probably some kids will actually think that way. I told you—these are not your usual kids. They—well, they are prepared to find art where other people find, um, like, a lack of skill or something."

"They ought to come to some of our hockey games, then," says Zip.

"You play hockey? Cool!"

"Our team sucks, though," says Zip. "So it's not all *that* cool."

"So, what do you say?"

"When's this party?" I ask.

"Next Friday night."

"What time?"

"Starts at ten. Goes until probably two. No alcohol, you can tell your parents. School security guard outside and in, watching the clock and all that. Very cool."

"We can't," I say, but Zip says louder, "What do we get paid?"

The kid smiles. "You mean you won't play for

art's sake?" Then he says, "We can give you four hundred bucks."

I say, "We won't play for *hockey's* sake, unfortunately. We got a game at six A.M. Saturday."

Zip waves me off. "We suck anyway. So what if you and I are a little tired?" He grins at the kid. "We'll play for five hundred."

The kid shakes his head, like he can't believe it. "I'm getting hustled by a twelve-year-old. No, really—we got a budget. Four bills is it."

"Sorry," I say. "It's not the money, right, Zip? It's just we—"

"Deal," Zip says.

"Cool," says the guy. "I'll be in touch." He opens the door, then turns back. "Do you have a band name or something?"

"Yeah," said Zip. "You can call us Puck You Two."

The guy leaves.

"Zip!" I say. "What's your problem?"

He whacks out a sloppy roll on his floor tom. "Come on, Codes. It will be the coolest. Making noise for a bunch of art goofs for serious money!" He laughs. "Let's practice so we stay nice and natural. Wouldn't want to acquire any skills."

"We got a game at six. Against Bowie."

He smacks his snare. "The very same team who just beat Reston 11–1."

"Yeah, I know, and Reston beat us, so that means we'll lose, but you know it doesn't work like that. We're different since the Montrose game. you're different."

"Not so different I can't use two hundred dollars," he says. "And the team isn't so different it stands a chance against Bowie, even if we got to bed at *seven* o'clock Friday night." He puts his sticks down and looks at me.

"Seriously, Codes—it's not like we're going to skip the game or something. We'll just stay up late."

"More like all night. Have you ever played a hockey game after staying up all night?"

"Yes!" he says, laughing. "I'm a *goalie*, you moron. Goalies don't sleep before games. I twist and turn and groan and thrash around. Then I give up and get up and go downstairs with my Discman and listen to Bad Brains music until it's time to get psycho."

"That's not the same. You'll be wasted."

"Nah. I'll be *loose*. And, look, you don't exactly

have to work up a sweat at this gig either. You can probably sit on a stool and twang two chords the whole time. If you can learn two chords in ten days."

I put down a couple of fingers and play a loud one. It sounds like someone dropped a tray of food. It's great. I can't help smiling.

"See? You already learned one," says Zip, picking up his sticks and dinging a long line of beats on his big cymbal.

I twang again, but with another finger down. It sounds even raunchier. Zip smashes his cymbal and it's like a car getting hit. "We *are* the best," I say.

"We're a *band.*" He does a little press roll on his snare, or what passes for a press roll from Zip. "Hey. Cody." I look at him. He grins and says, "Puck you."

I smile back. Maybe it *would* be okay. "Puck You *Two*," I say.

"And who knows?" he says. "Maybe we'll be so chilled we'll beat Bowie."

hings really are different on the Wings now. Losing to the Montrose Bears, the best team probably on the East Coast, by only one goal scored in the last second had made us all feel pretty good. We'd played hard and concentrated the whole game, every player on every shift acting like we knew how to do it— making a lot of moves we never felt we could dare to try before because we sucked so bad and the other team was always five goals ahead and superior. When someone is kicking your butt in hockey, you can't help it, you feel they are bigger and better human beings and you are just some kind of insect. But even though this was Superteam, we were acting like equals, making passes faster, trying plays like what my dad, who is the coach, wants when he says, "Be creative. Hockey is the last sport where you can."

We would have been beaten worse if it hadn't

been for the Zipster. He was outrageous in goal; he saved our tail. It's true that goalies are basically *there* to be outrageous and save your tail, but Zip has never been this good for a whole game in his whole career, and in the two practices since, he has stayed just as tough. He and I have been on the same teams since we were five. By the time he was seven he was amazing everyone—reacting so quick, throwing his body around like he had been playing a lot longer. The trouble is, now he *has* been playing a lot longer, and he's basically never changed his game. When you're seven and you make three bodacious saves in three periods, everyone is happy with that. When you are ten or eleven, it's not enough just to make three bodacious saves or even six, if you also let in a few easy shots all the other goalies stop routinely because maybe they were not as flashy as you four years ago but have studied harder since.

The other thing is that for a while Zip was mad all the time and treated everyone like dirt. His best friend left the team before the season, but so what? It seemed like it had to be something worse than that, and worse than all the losing too. We were *all* losing, but everybody except Zip found a way to have a good time, and my dad handled things right, letting everybody play, letting every shift have its turn even when it meant our worst guys were on the ice against their best guys, kind of forcing us to find something to feel good about, so we felt good about being hockey players at least, and being together. The dudes are pretty good dudes.

Some of us talked sometimes about Zip being such a pain, but nobody knew what to do. Then we had that game with the Bears, the team Kenny had jumped to, and Zip played great, even though Kenny (who is awesome) made the play that led to the goal that beat us. Since then, Zip has relaxed off the ice and been tense on it, which is what a goalie ought to do but is the exact opposite of how it was. And now, the whole team feels like a whole team. Some guys who hated Zip have actually started to see he's not a bad guy.

On the way to hockey practice the night after we signed up for our music gig, my dad asks me if I think Zip is ready to accept some tips from a goalie coach yet.

"No," I say. "Not, like, *really* accept them. I

mean, you know he goes to camps and clinics and stuff, all the time. But he doesn't listen."

My father looks out the windshield. "And you don't think he's ready to listen now? To just some fundamentals of angle play, stuff like that? Maybe from Quentin Frost?"

Quentin Frost played in the NHL and now does radio for the Caps' games. So he's kind of cool. My dad knows him from some summer camp he ran in Boston like twenty years ago when Quentin Frost was a kid. "Maybe," I say. "But why would you do it now? Zip's playing incredible."

"That's a point," my dad says. "Maybe we'll wait."

"If I were you, I'd get in somebody to teach the defense to poke-check, instead of worrying about Zip."

"You can't teach somebody how to poke-check," he says. "A kid either has the instinct and guts to try it at just the right moment or he doesn't. Look at Ernie in the last game—he tried to poke every time someone skated in on him, but he missed and left himself extended and off balance and got beat."

"Well, at least you can teach them to stay back on their skates when they lean forward to poke."

"That's true," he says. "Thanks. I'll try to work that in tonight."

We don't talk any more about the team. He asks me what one of my new records is like and I sing him one of the funny dirty lines from it and he shakes his head like kids are nuts. People probably think the coach and his son who is on the team talk all the time behind the scenes, but we don't, much. My dad always said fathers shouldn't ever coach their sons, and the only reason he's my coach this year is that another coach left suddenly. Sometimes, not often, he will ask me a very specific question about how a particular player or the team might react to some idea he has, and I tell him. Sometimes I will moan to him about why doesn't he teach Billy to stay onside when we have an odd-man rush, or teach Prince to keep his stick on the ice when he's not in front of the net, but he never replies directly. He wants me to be just a dude on the team and that's what I want too, and that's how it is. Probably the things I moan to him about I would moan to him about if he were just my dad, not the coach. And I would never, like, tip him off about a player behind the player's back. He has to spot things for himself.

One time, I did get mad at him. It was maybe our third game or something, and we got killed as usual, but we'd had a chance in the second period to get within two goals if he had skipped a shift for what was the Spaz Line for that game, and put Boot and me and Prince on for a long shift. But he gave the Spaz Line their regular shift and they let in *three goals*. I asked him in the car why he was so freaking dense. I was sick of getting slaughtered.

He calmly said, "I set the lines and the shift order in front of everyone in the locker room, and we follow that through the whole game. That's how this team has to be played."

"Why?" I asked. "Everybody else, every other coach, switches things around in special situations. What's so special about our spazzes?"

He thought for a minute and said, "First, it's that we have a lot of them."

"So?"

"Think about it. In terms of keeping this a *team*."

I thought. "You mean, if you avoided the bad

players, you'd have to avoid so many, that like only about six of us would play much, and even if we did better, won more or lost less badly, the poor things would feel left out?"

"Something like that," he said.

"What about the six of *us*, though? Don't we deserve something for, like, how hard we have worked and stuff to become so much better than the spazzes?"

He sighed. "Well, if I handle things right, you'll get the 'something' you deserve."

"What? You're telling me it won't be ice time."

"No. It will be belonging to a happy team."

"Oh, goody," I said. "I'm going to get to be *happy* losing 18–3."

He smiled. "That's right. And maybe after a while you won't be losing 18–3. You'll just be losing 7–4."

"Then I'll *really* be happy, right?" But I knew he had a point. Word gets around about every team in the club, and teams in other clubs too, and all the time you hear how miserable the Howard Bantam A's are even though they are 12–1 in league play, or how the Wing Peewee B's all hate to come to the rink because they hate each other and hate their coach, or how there are "troubles" on this team or that one. My dad was right—there don't seem to be a lot of happy teams you hear about. Especially the ones that win a lot.

At practice later, it looks like winning a lot and staying chipper won't become a challenge we have to face anytime soon. People are concentrating, working hard and all, feeling good, and my dad is teaching great, but, still, there is a lot of messing up all over. Every time I look up, I see someone over-skate a puck or let a pass slip under his stick or wait too long to backskate on defense. I never say anything, of course, and my dad never acts disappointed. But still, it amazes me. To understand how some of my teammates can lack such ordinary skills, sometimes I have to go back in my mind a long time and remember that I didn't know how to do that thing once, that somebody taught me and I must have been lousy at it for a while but by now I don't even think about it. This can get depressing when it is a simple basic skill and I have just *had* it for *years* and I am only eleven. It makes it plain we are a long way from being half decent. Years. And, ha ha, we play Bowie Saturday.

Zip looks great during all the shooting drills. He plays mad, which is good. If you beat him, he calls you something really foul or nicks you with his stick, even though this is just practice. It is a good sign. Also, I notice that when he makes somebody else mad, usually one of the spazzes, the spaz tries harder. Hey, five years of this and it might make a difference.

We scrimmage the Peewee B's who use the other half of the ice at the same time we practice. We do this at least once a week for ten minutes at the end of practice. It's supposed to be the fun time, the big reward for going through drills for fifty minutes. But the Peewee B's are big, and they are always pissed off at the end of their practices because their coach is a mean little weasel who cusses them out all the time, and so they take it out on us every week. I am the smallest player on our team. They can't resist trying to wipe me out. I can really skate, so they never really hit me with their clumsy goon checks, but it distracts me. Today I score on the first shift, though, a high shot the goalie flinches from.

Their coach screams something really nasty at him, so of course when I'm skating back up ice the goalie nails me in the ankle with the corner of his stick. It catches me just right and it hurts and I go down with a yelp.

I hear some grunting and yelling, so I look while I lie on the ice and see Woodsie kneeling on the goalie's chest and pounding him in the mask with both gloves. One of their big defensemen skeets up with a spray and yanks Woodsie off easily and puts both hands on his stick so he can slash Woodsie, but before he can do it Woodsie absolutely *slugs* him, right under the chin of his face shield, and the guy's skates lift off the ice an inch and he falls down. Then their fast little high-scoring winger who is a total chickenhearted wimp skates up full speed and cross-checks Woodsie hard from behind and he smacks into the crossbar, but Prince skates in and hooks the winger's skates, and gives him a perfect elbow to the helmet as he goes down. Before you know it, fights have broken out all over and we use up all the scrimmage time and the Zamboni man is blowing his horn because he has to resurface before the next practice and he *hates* it when kids even *dawdle*, but now there are all these brawls. Finally he drives out anyway, which gets everyone's attention because Zambonis are *big* and *loud* and you do not want to get run over by one, so it all breaks up and both teams make it to their locker rooms without fighting off the ice any.

Nobody is hurt by any of the fighting, of course, because we all wear so much stupid equipment, except my ankle and Woodsie's wrist, which he jammed when he was checked into the crossbar. We are all laughing and fake-slugging and everybody is cheering Woodsie because he flat knocked that defenseman *down*. Woodsie is pretty tall, and in his pads he looks decent-sized, but he is incredibly skinny and this kid could have swatted him away like a beetle if he hadn't been so busy getting ready to slash. Prince gets cheered a lot too, because everybody hates that little winger. He scores at least three goals every scrimmage against us and he celebrates them all by pumping his arm while sliding on one knee, and sometimes he even holds up the blade of his stick and blows on it because, see, it's just so *hot*, get it? Prince, who always responds to everything by singing phrases from songs no one else has ever heard, stands on a bench and lets go with a whole verse about champagne and diamonds.

"Hey," says Zip from behind me, kind of quiet.

"Yeah?"

He nods at Prince. "You want to sign up a vocalist for next Friday?"

"No way," I say. "First of all, that guy seemed to like it fine as just us two. Second, what is Prince going to sing *to*? It's not like we play songs. Third, he has a great voice and he's completely on key—"

"That's just it," Zip says, lifting off a leg pad. "Against our noise, that sweet sound would be just the coolest. And he could sing the crap he always sings. He seems to know hundreds of tunes with weird words."

"I think they must all be old stuff, *real* old. Like he learns them from his grandfather's 78s or something."

"Whatever."

I shake my head. "We'll wreck the whole first line for the game." Zip doesn't seem especially worried about that, so I add, "Plus we'll have to split the money."

"Maybe we better think a little more about it," he says quickly, and bends back to his other pad.

My dad walks in and watches for a minute, smiling, then he says, "Okay, listen up." Everyone calms down a little.

"First of all, Woodsie—that was perhaps a *slight* overreaction to a completely customary tap from a goalie who's just been scored upon in a practice scrimmage—"

Voices holler in protest, but Coach goes on.

"*However*, I appreciate your instinct to protect our wee precious little scoring machine when he went down like he was dead from the slight tap—"

"Kiss my socks," I say.

"And as for the rest of you"—he pauses, one hand held up—"free drinks."

Everyone cheers. The door opens and a couple of dads come in with their arms loaded up with cans. They walk around and every kid grabs a Coke or Dr Pepper or something. They get to Billy last and the only things left are two Mountain Dews. "Hey," he whines, "I don't like Mountain Dew."

"Then try my spit," says Dooby, hawking deep

in his throat. "At the moment it ought to taste a lot like Dr Pepper."

Billy's dad whirls around, but Ernie hands Billy a Coke and takes both Mountain Dews. "Thanks," says Billy.

"No problem," says Ernie. He guzzles, pauses to belch loudly, then finishes the first Dew with another swallow. He pops the second and drinks it all down in one pretty quick chug.

"Time to go," I say, picking up my bag and heading for the door. "Any minute now, all that fizz is bound to come out of *somewhere*."

On the drive home my dad stops at the 7-Eleven and buys me two donuts I didn't even ask for. I guess he's feeling good about the way the team jumped on the Peewees. I saw that the other coach was completely pissed, and when we walked by their locker room I could hear him screaming at them.

"That coach is such a jerk."

My dad smiles. "You know what he accused me of?"

"What?"

"Setting it all up: If we get a lead, we fight until

the Zamboni. That way we win."

"Hey! We *did* win! That's the first time we ever beat those huge stupid suckers."

"It was a nice goal, by the way."

I shrug. "He flinched, or he might have stopped it."

"That reminds me. Did you see how Zip took those three or four shots right in the mask last week? Those Bears came out shooting for the ol' melon, I do believe."

I laugh. "From the first time they came in our zone, he was sticking his head out and screaming, *'Feed me! Feed me!'* and opening his mouth behind his cage."

"Ah, the Zipster." He smiles out the windshield for a while. Then, with a kind of excitement I haven't heard in a long time, but real held back, he says, "If he's sharp on Saturday, and if you're skating hot and can get two or three, and if the D plays physical, we could beat Bowie. With you guys really *on*, we could *beat* them."

"Wow. That would be cool," I say. But I'm looking out the side window and feeling suddenly pretty uncomfortable.

## three

'm just plugging in to my amp that night when the guy comes back into Zip's basement.

"Don't you ever knock?" Zip says, acting mad.

"Actually, no," says the guy with a smile. "Never." Zip laughs.

"Hey," I say. "Do you have a name, or what?"

He kind of studies me. Then he bows, hair swinging, and straightens up, and says, "Gentlemen, my name is Parker."

"What a yuppie-scum name," says Zip.

"Then it's appropriate," Parker says. "I'm definitely yuppie scum all the way. My father is an attorney and my mother is a surgeon. What are your names? No doubt you too are yuppie scum; no one but yuppie scum is allowed to live in this development."

"I'm Cody." He nods at me.

"I'm Zip." Zip won't meet his eye. The kid raises

his eyebrows and looks back at me.

"His real name is Zachary."

"I'll kill you, Cody!"

Parker laughs. "Zachary! And I bet when you were two all your clothes came from Baby Gap."

"Okay, okay," says Zip all sulky.

"You started it," Parker reminds him. "Anyway—pleased to meet you."

"Are you going to be a poet or something?" I ask.

He makes a fake wince. "Oooh. No. Poets." He frowns and shakes his head.

"What do you do for the literary magazine, then?"

"I sell advertising and set up the printing. I don't do anything literary. Or musical. Nor do I paint." Then he says, "Hey, if you'd like to see the space ahead of time, I can arrange it."

"Are bands supposed to call elementary school cafeterias 'the space'?" asks Zip. "Or is that just an arty-punk thing?"

"It's a band thing," Parker says. "Get used to it."

"Will his drums fit on the stage?" I ask. Parker nods. "And my crappy little amp—is there an electric plug?" He nods again. "Okay," I say. "Then we don't need to see the space."

"What about a sound check?" Parker asks.

"A what?"

"Setting up early and playing a few songs so that you can adjust the acoustics just right."

"Forget it," says Zip. "It's going to be pretty hard for us even to figure out a way to sneak out of our houses and get there by ten."

"Would you like me to talk to your parents? I'll change clothes when I come to call."

"Or at least your boots. Though actually," I add, "those boots rule."

"You better not come," says Zip. "See, it's not that they wouldn't let us go and play music. Our parents are pretty cool. That's not the problem."

"But, see, my father is also our hockey coach," I say.

"Ah," Parker says. "And there's that absurdly early game."

Zip scoffs, "Our first year as Mites, every game was at 5:15 on Sunday morning." He puffs out his chest. "Hockey players are not sleep-wussies. No such thing as absurdly early for *us*."

"Pardon me for asking—I'm certain you're both very important in the team's scheme—but will success in the game hinge upon the two of you playing your best?"

"I'll be playing goalie against a very high-scoring team," Zip says, "and Mr. Clapton over there, as our team's best skater and highest scorer by a margin of two-to-one, will be expected to produce a brilliant offensive effort." Zip smiles. "We're probably counting on him for at least three goals. Plus he'll be smallest man on the ice, so he'll get hammered a lot."

Parker looks at me, kind of worried. "So are you guys going to really blow it for your team?"

"We don't plan on letting the gig affect us," I say.

"Except to make us feel all artistically stimulated and alert to creative subtleties," Zip adds.

"Well, good," says Parker. He takes out an index card and hands it to me. "Here's my address and phone number. See you later, then." And he leaves.

As soon as the door shuts, Zip starts a pretty even sort of classic rock beat, hitting his snare every other beat and his bass every beat and tapping a line on his hi-hat. I start playing just one string, one of the ones in the middle, moving my pick up and down. Then I find the string with my left hand and start moving it up, one fret to the next, skip a couple, go back down three, slide up real high . . .

"The Ventures' six best songs all at once on one string, as interpreted by hearing-challenged Germans who never saw surf in their life!" screams Zip. He tries to throw in a quick, tight tom-tom-to-tom-tom roll and messes it up a little and then can't get the beat going again right, so I start with some of my whang chords and he stops looking for that beat and fools around with his floor tom and his bass drum, getting this real low thing going. I try sliding my left hand up my three lowest strings and sawing at them with my pick and it sounds pretty cool for a while.

Eventually we stop and I pack up.

As I walk home with my guitar and my cheesy amp, it occurs to me to wonder what my parents would think about how I am using the guitar I asked for, which they bought me, and the amp. I don't play at home much, and when I do I usually don't bother to set up the amp, which I'm only allowed to use in a room in the basement that's practically soundproof. Playing a solid-body electric without an amp means no one hears what you're doing, not even you. So basically my parents gave me this big gift and they haven't ever heard what I'm doing with it. That's how they are, though. They probably figure I'm having fun with it *some* way, and that makes it okay. They've offered a couple of times to get me lessons if I want and I said no thanks, not yet.

Thinking about this makes me think about myself a little too. When I wanted the guitar, I had the idea I would learn how to play it all proper, and start a band, maybe with Zip if he ever learned to play his drums right. (He *did* have lessons two years ago, for about three months, but he quit.) I can learn stuff pretty easy. I learned how to play hockey and now I'm very good. Same with lacrosse, which I play in the spring. But when I think back to how it felt when I started hockey, it feels just like that with the guitar now. It felt like I was just playing around, and cool stuff started to happen, and I didn't think much about it when I was off the ice, and when I was doing it I was just doing it and not thinking about it either. Somehow stuff gets learned or sinks in or something. So why worry about guitar? This junk we play is fun. Somewhere along the line I'll probably start getting deeper into something with it. No hurry. Seems like eventually I get pretty good at whatever it is, and by then I'm doing all these things without thinking, *smart* things, so you might think I was analyzing, but it's not by brain. Coaches are always saying, "Way to think out there, Cody." It's more like, "Way to just go and play."

When I walk in the kitchen door my mom looks up from a pile of typewritten papers she's leaning over on the kitchen table, probably one of her students' theses or something, and she sees the guitar, and says, "Have fun?"

"Yeah."

She looks back down and keeps reading. "Playing with Zip?"

"Yeah."

She turns a page. My mom can read while she's talking to you but you know she's paying attention to you mainly. "I've always wondered if he was any good on those drums. Kathleen told me he quit his lessons a long time ago, but she also told me they got him a new drum for Christmas, hoping he was still interested. She says he found it and is using it already, which gives her the idea he likes playing, at least." She turns another page, and sighs at something in the writing.

"He does. He likes it a lot. He plays okay, I guess. He kind of has a few things he does really well, and he doesn't seem interested in getting the whole thing organized, but . . ." I shrug.

She smiles as she turns another page. "Sounds like the goalie I know."

"I guess. Yeah, you're right. What's for dinner?"

"Your father made chowder." She nods toward a big covered pot on the stove. Then she looks at me with a funny smile. "What's the matter with you? Can't you smell it?"

I sniff. I smell it. "Well, we were *talking*," I say. "You can't talk and smell at the same *time*."

She shakes her head and laughs and tells me to go start my homework.

## four

**M**y dad is a salesman. He works for himself, but he represents a whole bunch of companies that make weird medical devices, which he goes around and gets hospitals and doctors to buy. He must make a decent amount of money from selling only one of them now and then, because he never seems to be spending all that much time working his job. I think the machines cost as much as, like, satellites or something, so if he gets a little piece of the action he's okay. As long as I can remember, he's always been around the house for at least part of most days, and I've only seen him wear a tie three times in his life.

One of the things he does sometimes is get an actual sample machine to take around and flash in front of the people who might need such a thing. Most of the sample machines are just metal boxes, maybe with dials and gauges or whatever, but once in a while he gets something that looks like it just fell off a Martian spaceship, with bizarre nozzles and strange tubes and crazy complicated moving parts made out of strips of metal that hook together and bend with incredible precision. When he gets one of these, he will announce at dinner that we are going to play "Guess the Function!" and then later in the evening my brother Jerry and my mom and I sit in the living room and he brings the thing in, and we get to fool around and make it do things and then invent wacky ideas of what it's supposed to contribute to human health.

Tonight, while we eat his chowder and some biscuits Jerry made, my dad makes the announcement. Later, when we're all ready, he and Jerry go out to his truck and haul in this unbelievable piece of work. They are both grunting and saying "Got it okay?" to each other, so I guess some part of it must be full of mercury or something. When they put it down, my mother says, "Goodness!" and Jerry pants and my dad smiles down at the thing proudly, like he knows we will *never* get *this* one. It has a kind of dull pink metal base shaped like a stop-sign with angled sides that have tiny holes in some and these scary-looking sharp three-bladed knives coming out of others, and then the top, which is mostly made of blue glass, shows a coil of what looks like a foil hose inside, but out of four places come these bright green stiff tubes ending in black sacs with little gauges embedded right into the rubber. There's more, too, but that's the general picture.

"It's the best ever," I say.

"I don't know," says my mom. "I'm not sure it has the menace and complexity of that one we had last Christmas Eve, the blood-sugar-isotope-oscillator-spectroscope or whatever it was."

"Sold three of those to the NIH," says my dad. "That *was* a good 'un."

Jerry jumps right in and starts fooling with this thing, tweaking and yanking and bending, but aside from kneeling and touching the pink metal—which isn't *painted* pink, it's just pink all the way through—with one finger, my mom just sits back and watches. So do I.

She looks over. "Aren't you going to examine the specimen?"

I shake my head. "I've already figured it out.

Plus I'm kind of scared of those knives."

Jerry touches one of the blades, just to show *he* doesn't care, and he cuts himself, but nobody sees but me. My dad says, "You want to take your guess already?"

I nod, and sit forward on my chair. "Now, I have to tell you, this machine's use is very specialized," I warn them. This is, like, our most common joke. The uses of these machines are *always* very specialized. Sometimes there will be a hundred-pound thing that must have two hundred moving parts and costs $1.6 million and its purpose is to measure one amino acid present in tissue samples of people suffering from a disease that strikes between twenty and forty humans a year in the whole world.

"Okay," says my dad. "So it's not like a scale to weigh yourself on, or anything like that."

"Nope."

"What do the blades do?" Jerry asks.

I look at him. "They keep enemies away. By the way, they've been electroplated with a rare nerve poison." He looks worried for about two seconds, then grins.

"So what is it?" asks my mom.

I clear my throat and look out at them very assured and serious. "Once every eleven years," I say, "in states of the northern Midwest, such as Wisconsin and Minnesota, a child, aged *exactly* six, who has shown exceptional promise—*exceptional*, now—at playing goal in ice hockey, has the top half of his body cleanly sheared off by a huge snow-blower while he's playing in a drift of roadside snow." I nod at the machine. "This," I say, "is quickly transplanted directly onto his hips, and becomes the upper part of his body. Its various appendages are designed to allow the child to continue to develop his goaltending ability, so that he can live a nearly normal life, and fully enjoy the self-esteem that, as a star athlete, he so rightfully deserves. The hose inside the blue glass is a kind of cyberbrain," I add, "and the knives keep guys from skating into the crease for rebounds."

My mother says "Bravo!" and my father and Jerry laugh. Then, looking serious, my mother asks if she may pose a question to nail down a point about "specialization."

"Sure."

"If this rather horrible but—fortunately—

completely fixable accident happens only once every eleven years to a six-year-old of *exceptional* ability—and that indeed makes the use of this item *very* specialized—then may I ask how often slightly *less* talented goalies are chopped in two, and why the machine isn't used to assist them in their quest for self-esteem as well?"

"To ordinary goalie prospects it happens three times a week," I say. "So you can see it would just be too expensive to waste on mediocre talent."

Jerry comes up with a pretty wacky guess too, and we laugh a lot at that, and my mother makes up something about a filtration system for molecules created in the air by digital replay of recorded music by Hungarian composers who wrote viola sonatas in the eighteenth century, and finally my dad tells us what it's for but I can't really follow. Something boring, all about the endocrine system. Then my mom looks at her watch and says, "Okay, Cody. Bed."

As I start up the stairs, my father, who with Jerry is bending over to lift the thing back up and take it out to the truck, says, "Hey, Codes, think maybe we should keep this?"

I stop on the stair. "What for?"

"Oh, I don't know—just in case Zip loses a little of his quickness," he says. "I know a couple of surgeons who could fix him up with this unit and have him back on the ice in six hours."

"Why would Zip lose some of his quickness?" I ask, too fast.

My father looks at me a little funny. "I wasn't serious, Cody. It was a joke—the whole thing. I'm not worried about Zip's quickness."

"Sure," I say, with a big laugh. "Ha ha. Well, good night." I go upstairs. But it takes me a long time to get to sleep. When you're tired, quickness is the first thing to go.

## five

The next day I decide to go over to Zip's after school but before hockey practice, so we can play a little. When I walk in the basement door, I stop dead. Zip is sitting behind the drums, which is okay. But kneeling on the floor, carefully taking a microphone out of a case, is Prince.

He looks up and smiles. "Yo, Codes. Hey, close the door."

I bump it shut behind me, staring at Zip. He shrugs. "Prince came home from school with me so he could get a ride to practice." I look down at the mike, which Prince has removed and is attaching to a long cord. Then I look back at Zip. He squirms a little and says, "Well, I thought we kind of agreed it would be really cool to, like, have a singer."

"Can I just plug in to your amp, Code? I don't do anything very loud."

"Sure," I say. He takes the amp from my hand

and plugs it in and switches it on. "Um, like, welcome to the band, I guess."

"Thanks, man." He's lightly tapping the mike's top, looking at the amp's controls. "Lucky it's the day I take my microphone home."

"You keep a mike at school?" I ask.

He nods, a little embarrassed. "Um, I'm kind of in the school band. They do some numbers I kind of sing on. We have practice three days a week. And"—he looks even more embarrassed here—"I'm kind of picky about what kind of microphone I use, so I bring my own."

I don't ask why he has one in the first place. Probably for the same reason I have a guitar and Zip has drums. Instead, I say, "Listen, Prince. Did Zip happen to mention the date of this little concert of ours?"

Prince looks up at me, half wary, half innocent, trying to read how I feel about it. I don't show him anything. "Yeah," he says lightly. "Friday night. It's cool. I'm not doing anything Friday night. I mean, like, I had no other plans."

"Of course you didn't. You were going to go to bed early and *sleep*, to be ready for the Bowie game at six the next morning."

"Well," he says, looking down, "sure, of course, but, you know—"

I look at Zip. "You realize, of course, that now you have involved the team's *two* leading goal scorers, plus its best face-off man and best play-maker?"

"Jeez, thanks, Cody," Prince says. "Best play-maker, huh? I thought maybe Shinny was, but of course he's got that broken—"

I cut him off. "Prince, you shouldn't do this. It's bad enough already, just Zip and me. I mean, we're supposed to play until two A.M.! We're going to be tired!"

He looks me in the eye. "Then why are you going ahead and doing it?"

I stammer. "Well, if it's, you know, just me, oh, and Zip, well—"

"You can't have it both ways," Prince says. "Either it's a bad thing to do so *you* shouldn't be doing it, you of *all* people, Mr. Coach's Son *and* Best Player By Far, or, you guys decided it wouldn't really make any difference at all in how you play next morning, so you're doing it." He holds the mike to his mouth and through the amp comes his next comment in a loud whisper. "You think it won't matter, so I get to think that, too."

"He's right," says Zip. "So let's get playin'."

"The whole thing's wrong," I kind of mutter, but I get my guitar out and plug in anyway. I twang a couple of strings and we get the volume set at the right level. Prince is holding his mike, ready. "Um, P-man," I say, "did Zip, like, tell you what kind of— I mean, did he tell you, like, what we do? Or maybe I should say, what we *don't* do. Like play chords and tunes and beats or anything that resembles music."

Prince nods. "I got some ideas," he says. "Let's get it."

Zip clacks his sticks. "One, two—"

I fix three of the fingers of my left hand about midway up the neck, give a sigh, and start slashing with my pick. It sounds high and low at the same time, very fuzzy, very big. Very good. Zip thrashes at his snare so you can't even hear the individual strokes. Prince bobs his head, saying, "Yeah!" and "All right!" a couple of times, tapping his thigh with one hand as if there were some beat he could hear. Then he lifts the mike, closes his eyes, and lets out this incredibly beautiful high wail that sounds like something between a clarinet and an owl. It's so surprising and so pretty I almost stop playing, but then I notice part of the reason it sounds so good is that I *am* playing underneath it, so I keep at it. After a minute I slide my hand and press a couple of different strings, getting a much lower kind of boomy tone going. Zip switches to a slow-motion roll on his tom-toms, and Prince, like it was rehearsed, slides the wail note right into the first line of a song about love and sorrow and letters in the sand and stuff. He sings the whole thing, in perfect tune, perfect rhythm sustained the whole way through, a very nice melody it is too, though Zip and I change what *we're* doing eight or nine times each in every direction before he finishes. We all stop about the same time.

"Jeez," I say.

"*Yowsah!*" Zip howls.

Prince just kind of laughs softly, "Heh-heh," and says, "Oh my yes," and "That was *very* interesting, gentlemen."

"It certainly was," says another voice. We all turn and see that Parker has come in while we were playing. He's smiling and staring at Prince. Then he nods to Zip and me and walks over and shakes Prince's hand. "I'm Parker," he says. "And you're incredible."

"Thanks," says Prince.

"His name is something like Jawallah, but because he's the only black kid on the team and the rest of us are racist stereotyping pigs, we call him Prince," says Zip.

Prince nods. "It's okay," he tells Parker. "When we were Mites we had a Vietnamese player for one season and we all called him Sushi."

Parker says, "I can see that ice hockey is an arena in which political correctness has yet to get a toehold. All right. Prince it is. Besides, the singer who used to call himself that doesn't anymore, anyway."

"He's good, though. But he makes too many records."

"I agree. Nobody's *that* good."

"Prince knows lots of weird songs no one else has ever heard of, and mostly he sings them instead of talking to us in the locker room," I explain.

"I recognize that last song," says Parker. "I don't remember the title, but it's on this CD my father keeps at our house for when his dad comes to visit. It's all songs from the 1920s and the Swing Era and such."

Prince nods. "My grandfather was a singer in jazz big bands."

"Cody was kind of right," Zip says. "He said you probably got them from your granddaddy's 78s."

Prince shakes his head. "Nope. Straight from the man himself."

"Cool," says Parker.

"But won't singing like that wear you out?" I ask. "I mean, it must take a lot of energy—"

"No sweat." Prince grins. "I got lungs like you got legs, Codes. I sing more than you have skated in your whole life." He pats me on the shoulder. "I'll save plenty for that game, don't you worry."

But I do.

## SIX

t practice, Prince and Zip live up to their claim that the music isn't taking anything out of them. We spend the whole time in a half-ice scrimmage with full checking, and both guys play pretty incredible. Prince is wheeling through the zone away from the defense like he had discovered a special technique for accelerating, or he's skating untouched down the high slot with the puck and dishing backhand or forehand to his wingers at the last possible minute as he draws the defense to him. One of his wingers is me, and he sets me up all alone at the left post at least four times. I only get one past Zip, though, because Zip is playing absolutely unconscious. Nobody else scores on him the whole time.

We'd never spent a whole practice scrimmaging before. Coach almost never stops the play, not even when somebody does something my dad could have used as the basis for a quick lecture. I guess he just wants us to play. He skates in and out of the action without interfering (he's an incredible skater), watching, serious, saying pretty much nothing, just "Nice flip, Princer, right over his stick" or "Good skate save, Zip" or "Way to drift into the open spots, Boot" in a nice, low voice.

We don't stop to do the whole-ice thing with the Peewees. By the time the Zamboni man knocks on the glass and Coach waves and tells us to skate until he knocks again, we are flying and used to it. Checks, which are technically illegal until December first at this age level, are delivered for real, but the guy knocked down always pops up, eyes scanning for the puck, stick on the ice, eager. That's good. The wrist shots are hard and low and aimed, instead of being sloppy slappers taken just for the sake of looking like a Real Hockey Player.

Zip cusses, then he taunts, then he cusses. I know he's getting some bruises. He loves it. One time, when he stopped me point-blank and then stopped me on the rebound with his glove, he looked in my eyes and I swear he didn't recognize me as anybody he had ever met in his life as he said, "You shoot like milk tastes, you pitiful doot."

It was pretty cool.

In the locker room you can tell everybody feels good, but nobody's joking around much. It's different. Everybody is looking kind of grim and surprised, like they aren't sure but *maybe* they kind of think *someday* we *maybe* could put a couple of minutes of actual *hockey* together. There were plenty of mess-ups by the spazzy players, but if a guy fanned on a shot or let a perfect pass dink off his stick, somebody else just plucked it up fast and started another play, not pausing long enough even to let the spaz think "Oh, crap, I did it again." I look around the locker room at everybody's face. What I see is that nobody thinks he sucked. I wonder—it *feels* like this—whether that would translate into nobody thinking *we* sucked. That's probably going too far.

Coach comes in only for a second. He sees what's going on and doesn't want to mess it up, so he just says, in a quieter voice than usual, "We can play like that Saturday morning." Then he leaves.

In the truck, on the way home, my dad seems real serious, looking out the windshield. Twice he turns and starts to ask me something but decides he won't just yet. Finally, without turning to me, he says, "The funny thing is, it's almost there. I mean, not everything, nothing that would make us suddenly a fabulous winning team, but—*something*, something we're close to getting, that will make us a team that . . . that refuses to believe we're going to get beat until somebody *proves* it and when they beat us they will almost wish they hadn't. And then next game we refuse all over again. That's how tough and happy we could be. That kind of team scraps and hustles and even wins a few, even without the most consistent skills in the world." He shakes his head and smiles. "We had some stuff going out there today."

"What's missing? Aside from talent?" I ask him.

"Now, hey, we've got some talent. We might even have just barely *enough* talent, if we—" He thinks. "If we were just all together, if something just put us all in one feeling and thinking groove, the talent we have, from you and Prince and Dooby and Zip and even Billy, would stretch to everybody, the way it's already stretched to someone like Woodsie. Just get in that groove *once* and it would be enough and we wouldn't let it go. It might not even have to be a hockey thing."

"So take us on a field trip to the Smithsonian on a bus or something."

He looks at me, mad. "Don't."

"I'm sorry," I say. "I guess I didn't know if you were, like, really serious. I never heard you talk like a sports TV-movie before."

He smiles, not mad anymore. "I know. I catch myself thinking in language that sounds like—what do they call it?—New Age or something, all the time now." He shakes his head, rubs his face with a hand. "I don't mind telling you, this is a challenging team to coach."

"I imagine so." We're quiet for a minute. I'm thinking.

Finally, I decide to say it. "I guess I kind of wonder why you're bothering to, like, try to *go* someplace with this team. Wouldn't it be a lot easier just to set the shifts, let the good kids try to have fun doing their skill things, let the spazzes feel bad at first and then good when they finally do a couple of things right by the end of the season, half because you taught them and half because some things just finally sank in from all that ice time?"

I look at him. "Look, I haven't talked with any-body, not at all, about this—kids don't talk about this stuff, you probably know. But, as a player, I've kind of gathered that's what you decided to do, and, from just kind of looking around, I think everybody else has figured out the same thing and come around to thinking, 'Well, okay.' So, you know, you *could* just let it slide. It's true we prob-ably won't be losing by ten, twelve goals by the end of the year, except to a couple of Pennsylvania teams. It's true I'll probably get fifty or sixty goals, and Prince will get maybe twenty-five and prob-ably sixty assists. Boot will score plenty, of course, don't worry. Dooby and Barry will get plenty of chances to be heroic defensemen—I mean, they ought to be happy, they're seeing more action, more three-on-twos, than the D on a good team ever sees. Ernie will be solid, minor but solid. If Shinny comes back, he'll be clever with the puck as usual. You mention Billy. Yeah, he skates pretty, he shoots pretty, talent, okay, but he's a zero. Maybe you're going to try to surgically detach him from his dad or something, maybe he's your, like, 'project.' The only player I see anything cool happening with is Woodsie. I mean, it's like every two games he's played a whole season and learned that much in between. I'd rather play with him passing to me almost than Prince, and he's learning to hit people too and he loves it. The rest are total losses. And, of course, now all of a sudden Zip is the greatest, but that could change too."

It's the most I have ever said, the most I am *going* to say, and he's trying to decide whether maybe it's enough. After a while he decides it's not.

"Do you remember the last time I 'coached' you?"

"Sure. You started that, like, clinic for little kids, when I was, what, four?"

"Four." He nods. "And who else was in that clinic? Getting their very first taste of skating and ice hockey?"

I think for a second. "Zip, of course. Dooby. Kenny Moseby. Pelletier, but he was jerk even then, and he quit because he knew nobody liked him. Boot—or was he the next year? Barry. He came partway through and stayed. A couple of kids I can't remember because I haven't seen them playing anywhere around here. You did it the next year, too, and Prince came, but then halfway through you handed us over to Coach Kay and we played a few games and stuff."

He downshifts, makes a turn, gets going fast again, and shifts up. "And that same group, give or take a couple, has been the core of every team you've played on, right?"

"Right. All travel, starting with Mites."

"Different coaches."

"Oh, sure. Every season."

"So," he says, turning in to our development. "So I take these little weenies who collect Ninja Turtles and listen to Raffi tapes, and I get to see them start off together as hockey players. Then, for seven years, seven seasons of thirty, fifty games each, I watch other men coach them. Coach *my* weenies. Only they don't stay weenies long, do they? Prince grows eyes in the back of his head and sees the ice better than his coaches, Barry decides only wimps score goals and real men just stop other people from doing it, Dooby and you start to skate better than players twice your age—"

"Okay," I say, a little uncomfortable. "I get it.

Now you get to have us again. The big reunion."

"I've really kept it from feeling like that, haven't I? For you guys?"

"No question. None of us ever thought of it, I bet. For us, it's just hockey with the Wings, ho-hum, another season, another coach, like that. Sorry if that hurts your feelings," I add.

He smiles. "It doesn't. It's how I wanted it. Of course, I haven't been entirely able to keep *myself* from feeling the reunion thing a little, but I've tried to control that too. But tell me this: In all of those other seasons, going all the way back to before Mites even, did you ever play on a losing team?"

I think. "No."

"In fact, you won a lot. Sometimes—several times—you were the champs."

I nod.

"But now that you're playing under *my* coaching . . ."

"Well, come on. I mean, some kids left, okay? I mean, be fair. You got loaded down with a team that's half complete hockey gremlins. We got no business playing as an A team, but that's what we all wanted, and we voted for it. The parents wanted it too. That's not *your* fault. If we were B's maybe it'd look better to whatever dippy parents are complaining to make you feel bad now, but, hey, the *team*, the *guys*, we know how it is—we don't think you could do anything."

We're on our street now, and he pulls in to our driveway and turns off the motor but makes no move to get out. "Well," he says, "thanks, of course—I mean, I'm glad the team sees it the way it is. I've been coaching hockey now for nineteen years at one level or another, and I have enough experience and knowledge to know what I can and can't take care of." He looks at me with a smile. "Which brings us back to the start of this talk: All my experience tells me something could happen with this team. Something that would not look like anything much to anybody outside the locker room, but something everybody else—the players— would know, and take on the ice, and take into next year."

I open my door before he can start expressing his hope that it would all come together in the Bowie game day after tomorrow, when, as far as I can see, three of the players he is most counting on will be dragging their butts from playing non-music all night long. "Well, everybody's pretty happy already," I say, sounding stupid and too chipper. Then I hop out and close the door. But through the window as he half watches me and half thinks, I can see *Bowie, day after tomorrow!* in his mind.

**7** t got worse, *much* worse. After dinner, I hauled my guitar over to Zip's, reminding myself as I stood at the basement door not to be too shocked when I walked in and saw Prince and his pretty microphone. I sighed, cussed Zip, and opened the door.

"Hey, Codes!" says Dooby, holding a little saxophone and kind of bouncing on the balls of his feet.

"Hi, Cody," says Barry, holding a trombone and looking very embarrassed.

Prince nods hello and takes my amp, eager to get the electronics straight. I look for Zip, but the stool behind the drums is empty.

"What—"

"Well, the secret kind of leaked a little," Dooby says, "and me and Barry can backskate for sixty minutes on no sleep *any* day, and, well, there was a time when we thought we might start a funk band

and learned, like, a few old Funkadelic horn parts to kind of build on, and—"

"And that sounds like a strain of separate but equal non-melody we could use in the terrifying mix we're preparing to blast those poets with," says Zip, coming around the corner with a tray full of sodas.

"Um, I also play in the marching band," Barry adds, looking down at his trombone slide.

Suddenly it's like this weird little two-thing has become a party and Zip is the host. Everybody snatches a few gulps of cola and grabs some pretzel sticks from a bowl in the middle of the tray, and Zip takes his place behind the drums, and then everybody gets his instrument all set and then turns and looks at me.

"What?" I say.

Zip smiles and looks all around, then back at me. "We're waiting, I think, to see whether you foam at the mouth or play your guitar."

I look around. Prince nods, but I can't tell if it's to me or just in time with a beat he already hears. Barry looks out of the side of his eyes, like "Whatever you say, man, I don't want to make any trouble." It's Dooby I'm most surprised to see. He's the only person on the team who dares to snarl about stuff like "being a team" and "responsibility." And he's also too cool to care about *anything* off the ice. Yet here he is, possibly blowing a game, just to play his saxophone with the boys. He meets my look all serious for a minute, then just shrugs. "Might be fun, you know?" he says. "What's a little fun?"

I make a little frowning face, like I'm really thinking this tough one through. But meanwhile I'm letting my left fingers find some strings to pinch, and turning the volume knob on my guitar all the way up with my right thumb. Then, still frowning thoughtfully, without looking up, I slash at the strings with my pick, *shanggggg*, and again, *whongggggg*, and start playing the chords as hard as I can. Zip jumps in behind the third one with a cymbal crash and then a big snare roll leading to a kind of rock beat, and Prince is right behind with some falsetto "Ooooooh yessssss, ooooooooh yeah" stuff that leads into a long line of nonsense syllables and then a tune about a carriage ride 'neath the full moon. Dooby lets out kind of a squawk on his saxophone, then screeches a little as he finds his way to something like a copy of Prince's tune but nowhere near what you might call the same key, and then I start twanging my high string and Barry, flushing red, puffs out his cheeks and starts playing what sounds like five notes from some march, over and over again, the whole time, *oomp-wah-oomp-wah-wow*. We do at least twenty minutes without anybody even stopping to breathe, and it's like getting a look at the surface of Saturn.

When we suddenly stop, we all look at each other like, "Did that just happen? What was it? And was it really *that great*?"

That's when it occurs to me that maybe we *will* beat Bowie.

## eight

**B**efore I leave for school my dad says, "Cody, tell the boys I got some ice time tonight, fifty minutes at eight o'clock, anybody who can come. I got the *whole* ice. We'll scrimmage, if enough kids can come. I'll call the others who you won't see."

"Cool," I say. We never get to see the whole ice sheet except in games, which is what makes games so special, frankly. Two teams always divide it for practices, always. But while I feel myself get excited I also feel my stomach sink. I know what my dad has done: He's gone and shelled out two hundred bucks of his own money so we can have some fun and Maybe the Together Thing Will Happen. But right now I can still feel my body buzzing from all the music we made last night, and I realize I have come around to getting as stoked about this art-punk poetry dance as I am about the hockey game. This isn't what you want to feel if you are the coach's son, the big scorer, blah blah blah. Especially not if a guy like my dad—the very best— is the coach.

On the way to school I try to right myself, like I was walking off balance. But I keep remembering moments out of what happened last night, like this time when I decided to try to play the notes Barry was playing, and after a minute, just on one string, my bottom string, I did it—I matched him, and it made this kind of what I think they call harmony, different notes that sound good together instead of like a fight, and we kept it up and Barry—*Barry*—started bending his knees and kind of bobbing down and up, which is all I guess a trombone player can do to rock out. Or this time when Dooby got so wound up, or maybe it was just warmed up, that he broke through something that had been holding him back and all of a sudden he got *loud* and I just dropped out to let him wail, and Zip and Barry did too, only Prince staying with him, cutting the song he was singing and just going *"Ooooooooooo"* very high, trying to follow Doobs or lead him, I don't know, but it ruled.

So by the time I get to school and see Dooby

and Zip standing together on the playground talk-ing and waving their arms, I have not exactly turned myself back into Hockey Son. But I remember, then. And I slow down, and bring my mind back. Yeah, come on, Cody boy, remember the ice under your skates, the puck, the tape balls flying, hooray . . . And by the time I hook up with the two of them, I have pretty much come around.

"Hey, guys, guess what? My dad—"

Zip breaks in, grinning, his cheeks red with the cold, gesturing with his hands. "We were just, like, trying to figure out what we sounded like most of the time—"

"Yeah, and what we should name ourselves," says Dooby, also grinning, also gesturing. They look at each other and start laughing.

"The Brokemotorgrinds," says Zip.

"The Vomiting Whale," Dooby replies.

"Sweet Soul Boy and the Cracker Crunchers."

"The Random Polka Orchestra."

"Hog Suck."

"No, Hog Suck and the Spittles!"

They are passing back and forth, howling, shout-ing names, and I know I will never break straight in with hockey. So I laugh along too, and some of the names *are* pretty funny, and then I suggest one.

"No Bleeping Idea."

They both stop and look at me. "Whoa," says Zip, all serious.

"That's freaking *it*," says Dooby, all reverent.

"It says it *all*."

We all nod and smile and slap five. Then there's kind of a lull. I wait a few seconds, then say, "Oh, and guess what else cool? My dad, like, bought us some ice time tonight, and guess what?"

Their eyes are kind of refocusing, as hockey starts to emerge. "Um, what?" says Dooby.

I make myself grin. "He got us the *whole sheet*. And we're going to do nothing but scrimmage. End to end."

It only takes a second for Dooby to hook in. "Wow," he says, "the whole ice. Wow. Cool! I'll be able to swivel at the red line and build up some backskate speed when that little scooty Prince tries to fancy around me. And maybe there'll be some penalties and I can ice it backhand." Dooby is famed for this—grabbing the puck from around our goalie while the other team has a power play, then skating to the left corner along the goal line and lofting a backhander that sails over everybody's heads. They watch helplessly as it lands somewhere around the other blue line, maybe even in the zone, and they cuss and chase it and the parents go "Oooh!" One time when I saw him starting toward the corner I busted out of the zone and skated as hard as I could and got fifteen feet on the power-play defensemen and going full speed turned around just in time to see the puck saucering right toward me. I had to hold up one stride to let it land onside, then I took it in and flopped the goalie and lifted a backhand, shorthanded, and Dooby has never let me forget it was the greatest set-up I ever got.

"What will we use in the other goal?" says Zip. "That stupid board with the holes around it that none of you guys have ever figured out how to score through?" Zip hates to lose even scrimmages.

I'm glad we're talking hockey now. "Actually, Coach said something about asking Billy's father to strap on the pads."

They howl. "*Yess!*" says Zip. "Then I am *definitely* dressing out and playing center. I want to take some zingers at that sucker's melon." Billy's dad is generally not loved. Assisting on the bench during games, he has occasionally held back a kid going out for his shift and said in a low voice with a wink like he was cutting him a break, "Hey, let Billy take another couple runs; his Achilles has been a little tight" or some such crap, and Billy gets a double shift.

We wander into school talking about the scrimmage.

# nine

The scrimmage, for me, comes and goes in a blur. Maybe I'm not concentrating. Maybe it's just that when I get a crack at the whole length of the ice I tend to skate too much. But for the whole time it feels like I'm watching all these guys workin' hockey and I'm whizzing around the outside of their play. Sometimes, even when you're concentrating—sometimes *especially* when you're concentrating—the game feels like this, like it's a movie and you're seeing only every fifth second, and the four in between are completely dropped out. Sticks and skates and knees and elbows and ice, ice, ice, and, somewhere, anywhere, this puck that's always moving faster than your eyes and always heading out of reach in some other direction, except for when you don't see it coming and it hits you in the skates or glances off your hip and bounces to where someone else takes care of it.

Not everybody makes the scrimmage, so we pretty much get to go all the time instead of in shifts. This ought to be more fun, ought to let us get our rhythm going, try creative stuff. Prince plays pretty well again, dishing here, dishing there. Dooby lifts quite a few of his famous clears, and gets to show off his backskating as much as he wants, even when he should be going forwards. Barry is Barry—always solid and silent and exactly in the right purely defensive position. Zip is not as sharp as yesterday, and after he lets in a third goal from Boot he decides he's not mad anymore, now he's funny, so for the rest of the time he yowls and barks like a dog and calls everybody by someone else's name. He lets in a bunch more goals. I begin to get the idea maybe I'm not the only one who feels weird out here.

Coach blows the whistle when there's still maybe five minutes and I wait for him to say, "Okay, skate some lines and get off." Skating lines is considered a major pain, the usual punishment for when a team is a little slack. You start on the goal line and go hard to the blue and skeet to a stop and skate back and skeet, then skate hard to the red and stop, then back to the blue and stop, and so on, all supposedly fast as you can. I never mind much, because I'm a flashy skater and it's all just showing off. Everyone else hates it, though. But Coach doesn't tell us lines. Instead, he just says, "Okay, a good time was had by all; let's save something for the game," and off we go, early. Hey, nobody ever leaves a sheet of hockey ice early. The blank ice just sits there, waiting for the Zamboni, screaming in its dull white way that kids ought to be cutting it up.

The locker room feels maybe a tiny bit awkward, a little quiet, and not just because there are fewer of us. Everyone kind of hurries and gets dressed, talks but talks lower. Nobody does anything cranky or unusual, everybody's good-natured enough, but it sure doesn't feel like it did after that scrimmage yesterday. It's like people are saving their intensity, thinking of something else, and I'm afraid I know just what it is. I find out as soon as I get out in the hall and come up on a group that includes Dooby and Prince and Billy and a spaz forward called Shark because he never goes to the net and has rarely even shown the fact that he knows how one scores in hockey. He's an okay guy, pretty shy, works pretty hard, keeps his frustration to himself always. He's one of our four fat kids (Ernie is also heavy, though he can play pretty well, and Marshall is a tub but quick. Java's pretty round too.)

"Hey, Codes," Doober says, waving me into the circle. Prince greets me with, "The ax man, ready to chop," ax meaning your instrument, which seems a little risky to be saying in front of everyone. But then I notice Billy and Shark watching me carefully and I get a funny feeling. "Guess what?" Dooby goes on. "The No Bleeping Idea horn section just gained itself a couple of new voices."

"I play the trumpet," Billy says, eagerly. "I'm awesome, too."

Shark, who is very smart and always says things in weird ways, adds, "I follow the tradition of endomorphs in orchestral history who gravitate, ha ha, toward the thinnest instruments. In my case, I have been forced since the age of five to play the incredibly straining oboe."

I look at Dooby and Prince. They're smiling, pleased, everything's just dandy, didn't we do 'good'? I realize nobody really told them this was a secret, and since they blew off the idea that they were going to tire themselves out for the game, why should they hold back? I look at Billy. He's grinning, nodding like "Okay? Okay?," waiting for approval like he always is: "Am I one of the guys yet?" I look at Shark. He always seems a little bored and above it all, same as now, but his eyes are waiting, and I realize he wants to be included, it's important to him too.

"Well," I say, trying to smile convincingly but feeling pretty sunk after that funky scrimmage, "um, welcome to the band, I guess."

Billy pumps his arm and says "*Yesss!*" and Shark just leans his head in a little bow. I hold up my hand.

"But listen," I say, "and this goes for you two also," I say to Prince and Doobs. "This has gotten kind of out of hand. I mean, remember we're a hockey team, okay? That's who we are. And this hockey team has a game, against Bowie, who we all *ought* to know is Wolfbay's longest most hated rival, and we owe it to ourselves and our teammates and Coach too to be ready to play at the top of our game on Saturday. This music thing, it's more like a joke. So you have to promise me right now you won't tell anybody else about it, and between now and the gig you'll get all the rest you can."

They all get serious and say, "Sure, Codes, of course," and "No problem, no problem," and "Hey, no sweat, I'll be there hot to trot," and that sort of thing. Even Shark nods and says, "Be not concerned. I will get my Z's. Minor though my contribution is doomed to be, I make a point of preparing fully for each contest, in terms of rest, nutrition, and attitude."

I heave a sigh. "Okay, then." I start to go.

"When do we rehearse?" asks Billy.

"Bands don't 'rehearse,' you idiot," says Dooby.

"Especially not this band," says Prince. He looks at Billy and Shark and smiles. "It's more of a jammin' kind of thing. But don't worry—there's no way you won't fit in just fine." He grins at me and Dooby. "Am I right, bandmates?"

Dooby nods, but says, a little nervously, "Actually, we were kind of waiting for Zip to see if maybe we could go over to his place tonight for—"

"No," I say. "Absolutely not. Look, it's a school day tomorrow, we just played an hour of extra hockey, we won't even get home until long after nine, so listen." I point at them. "We all go home. We go to bed. We are hockey players. Tomorrow night, a little before ten, we'll all show up with our instruments at the cafeteria of Rocky Glen Elementary School, and *then* this music thing will just start. You'll have to work out how you're going to sneak out, on your own. But keep it *secret*. And leave it until tomorrow. Tonight, we're the Wolfbay Wings Squirt A's. And Saturday, as the Wolfbay Wings Squirt A's, we do the playing that *really* counts."

I sound mad, and so Dooby and Prince back up and say, "Sure, Codes, absolutely right" and "Lighten up—we're cool on the rest thing." Billy looks mystified, but I see Prince shoot him a wink, so he smiles and nods at me. Shark gives me a single honest nod.

But I feel like a complete fake when I climb into the truck beside my father. At the beginning of all this, it was just Zip and me, and I had not been such a strong team captain/coach's son/leader kind of guy then, all full of resistance and priorities and anger.

"Thanks for the ice," I say to my dad. He just nods and we drive out of the parking lot.

Nobody talks for a while. Finally, he says, "I guess I blew it. I thought maybe tonight was the extra thing we needed to pull it together, but instead it went away."

"No it didn't," I say.

He shrugs. "Got looser, anyway."

"It's a school day, an optional skate, not the whole team—it's bound to feel different."

He nods, but he doesn't believe me, and we don't talk until we're pulling into our driveway.

"Do me one favor," he says. "I would never ask you to spy for me or report to me or anything like that. You know that, right?" I nod. "But if you believe what we were talking about yesterday, and you think I'm about to blow it again, tell me. Okay?"

"You didn't blow anything," I say, "and you can't blow anything. You're the coach, and you're a great coach, and anything this team *has* it gets from you, so relax. Maybe you get your hopes up a little, that's all."

What a fake. And I always thought of myself as a pretty simple kid.

# *ten*

**W**hen I see Zip at school Friday morning he's pretty businesslike. He says Parker came by again, and they've worked out "the details," including how they're going to sneak Zip's drums and cymbals quietly out of his basement. Fortunately Zip's brother Scott has a late game in Annapolis tonight, and although right now only his dad is planning on going, so that his mom can watch Zip's early game on Saturday, he says he's pretty sure he can shame her into going to Scott's game too. Fortunately Parker drives, and even has access to a van. Zip says I can bring my stuff over this afternoon and they'll take it to the school for me. "Just be glad you don't play drums, man," he says, shaking his head. "I never had to think about *moving* the suckers before. It's going to take a couple of hours!"

"Have you talked to any of the others about how they're sneaking out?"

He shakes his head. "They're all big boys; they'll work it out."

"What about the fact that you share a room with Scott, so when he gets back from his game—"

"I, um, told my folks I was staying with you."

"What?"

He shrugs. "I'm spending the night at your house. So, you can ask your mom, I'll run back from loading the van with Parker, we'll go to bed nice and early, and then when we sneak back in at three or whenever, we'll just do it together. You have your own room, with a window and everything. It ought to be slick for us to get in and out of there."

School passes in smoke. Whenever I see a Wing/Idea guy, I nod seriously and keep walking. I have to admit, I'm getting excited as the day moves on. I mean, I *love* playing that music. But I don't want to talk about it. I guess partly I want almost to pretend it's just going to "happen." And almost, like, happen *to* me, as if I weren't involved. I'm not nervous at all about the music part, or the art-punks liking us; I'm nervous about the hockey, Bowie, and most of all, my dad.

School ends. I walk home, dreaming up what my fingers would look like making chords that sounded this way or that. Now that the music is the next thing, it's okay to think about it, as long as I'm careful around the house. When I get home, everyone is rushing out to one of Jerry's games. I wish him luck and make a sandwich and eat it and go and get my guitar and amp and stuff. When I leave the house, I pause at the door and think, *I'm leaving to play my first gig*. It makes me laugh.

I walk into Zip's basement. He's sitting behind his drums but not playing. He's biting his nails instead. Goalies are required to be nail-biters; I don't know about drummers. "Want to play?" he mutters, showing clearly he does *not* want to.

"No," I say. "Save it." I put my stuff near the door. Then I go over to his father's old record player, which he set up in the basement. It's great to have tunes down there, but the only trouble is, there are only old records. All the CDs are kept upstairs. So we got no Nirvana, no Foo Fighters, no Meat Puppets, no Nine Inch Nails. But there *is* a lot of cool old stuff that sounds all ancient and neat. I pick out a record without looking and put it on. It's the Grateful Dead. They're okay. Some of their stuff sounds kind of like me, in fact.

Zip, I can see, is really nervous. "Look," I say, "the worst thing that can happen as far as the music goes is that you forget the band's name and what it means. You have no idea now what's going to happen, what you're going to play, and so you're suddenly uncomfortable. But that's basically how you always play goal, and you do great there, right?"

"Sometimes I suck," he says.

"You're not the world's best technical drummer either," I admit. Then I shrug. "Don't get serious on me now, Zip. Save it for the game tomorrow. You and I have never done anything in this basement but goof around. That's all we're doing tonight, only other people will be goofing off with us too."

"You're right," he says, and hops down from his stool. He goes to the door and looks through the window. "I guess I'm not worried about playing these drums as much as *moving* them. Parker should be here soon."

I don't especially want to see Parker, so I discuss how Zip and I are going to meet later and slip "in for the night" and all that. Then I leave. I see a van turn onto the end of the next street over. Probably it's Parker and he and Zip are going to load across the backyard as soon as it's a little dark.

A couple of hours later, I'm sitting on our deck in the chilly air drinking a cherry Pepsi when I see someone coming, and it's Zip. Instead of walking up the steps, he climbs onto the railing and jumps down, landing softly on both feet, knees bent, hands out in karate-chop position, head swiveling as if to spot ninjas springing out from behind the barbecue grill.

"Looks like you're ready to sneak in," I say.

He stands up and comes over and grabs my Pepsi and swigs and hands it back, burps slightly, and says, "All set up. It's awesome."

"What? The cafeteria?"

"It's not a *cafeteria*, buttmunch. It's a *concert hall*. Or maybe a *club*. Yeah, a club. I'd rather be one of those music dudes who play in clubs where half the audience is dopes getting drunk and going off to puke in the bathroom and half is musicians come to study my astonishing technique."

"Where'd you get the technique? And is that what you brought instead of your pajamas?"

He pulls a toothbrush out from a back pocket of his jeans. "Details must be correct," he says. "And I don't sleep in pajamas, ever."

"You sure won't sleep in them tonight."

He's bouncing around the deck, all excited. "What's with you?" he says, stepping up onto a deck chair and hopping down backwards. "Aren't you, like, psyched for this?"

"Sure," I say. "But you know me."

"No, this isn't just the usual supercool one-thing-at-a-time-ho-hum-we'll-get-into-that-then Cody. You're a little tight, man. I can feel it." He puts his hands up to his temples. "Ugh. If you don't loosen up it's going to give me a headache and I might mess up some of that crucial rhythmic support you and our brother musicians need."

He drops down into the chair next to me and puts his elbows on his knees and looks at me. I meet his eyes. He puts his hand out and taps me a couple of times on the knee. "Hey, Codes. Your dad's the coach. You're not."

He leans back but is still looking me in the eye.

"I have a great idea. How about if right now you just *forget* the hockey game tomorrow, and live the way you always do, which is, 'Hey, look what's going on right here, cool!' Then you'll have fun tonight. And then, whoa, surprise! Tomorrow morning, a hockey game will pop up in front of you and, typical Cody, you'll charge into *that*. And play great. You love hockey, man, you know that—you'd play it anytime. So, okay, count on yourself to play it tomorrow. Tonight, just come inside with me and hang around your room for a while and then we'll take a walk, and, whoa! The chance to play some tunes on your gee-tar with the dudes might pop up."

I think about it. It's true I'm not acting like myself at all. "You're right," I say. "Screw this." I get up. "Let's sneak inside and, like, set up the scene of the crime."

"Bring your drink can," Zip whispers. "Evidence. Who knows what a sharp detective might do with that can?"

"My parents will never know. And they sure won't hire a detective."

But he's already inside, and I follow him. When

I get to my room he's got the computer on and is setting up a two-man kill game.

"I'm kicking your tail this time," he says.

"Oh, sure, okay." We play for a while and I whup him six in a row, so we switch to a geometry game that he's better at so he can win a few and feel better. Then he looks at a watch I've never seen him wear before and says, "Jeez. Time—" He raises his voice, even though everybody's still at Jerry's game. "—*Time to get ready for bed, Cody.*"

He leaves me to switch off the computer and goes to the bathroom, where he brushes his teeth for at least four times as long as he ever has when he's slept over, and then he insists I do the same, and then he makes us lie down and says, "*Good night now*," and we switch off the lamps.

"Lie here quiet for a while, then we'll stuff the beds to look like we're here if anyone peeks in," he whispers.

"No one will peek in. They leave me alone. My dad will come by at 4:30 and whack hard on the door until he hears me say, 'Ice hockey ice hockey ice hockey ice hockey ice hockey' five times, which means I'm really up, then he'll go downstairs and make coffee and I come down in a few minutes and we go."

"Will he expect me to say it too?"

"I don't know. You can just make some kind of noise that shows you're up, or I'll tell him you're up. Besides, so what if he looks in? We'll *be* here then. No doubt we'll look pretty sleepy anyway."

"No, we won't," he whispers. "We'll be primed and ready, full of the energy that comes from artistic achievement and loud funky music."

"Whatever."

In a few minutes he pops up, still insisting on whispering all the time, and we mess the room up a little and then we get some sweaters and things and make these body shapes in the beds. He insists we use real shoes for the feet parts. "Nothing else looks like a foot," he whispers. "A detective would look there first and see the legs just kind of taper off into nothing, and he'd know something was wrong."

"I keep telling you—"

"*Sssh*. Now, how are we going to get out of here?" Zip goes to the window.

"Well," I say, "nobody's home, so we could just walk out the back door. It always works for me."

"Don't be a dope," he whispers. "Besides, we have to, like, prepare a path for re-entry in the dark hours."

I walk over to the window and open it. My father hasn't put the storms on yet, fortunately. My mother will have to remind him for at least another month. I point past the screen. "We can climb out here, turn that little corner, and step onto the garage roof. It's a jump from there, but you can hang if it bothers you."

"Two things. One, can we get back *up* onto the garage roof? And, two, if we leave the screen off and the window just barely cracked, will anybody see?"

"We can put the screen back once we've climbed out. It'll look normal. I used to do this when I was little and Jerry was supposed to sit for me but he would just go down in the basement and work on his backhand with a tennis ball against the wall and ignore me after I was supposed to be asleep. I'd go out just before my parents got home and wait until they'd had time to come in. Back then, they *did* check on me. I wouldn't be there. I'd see my light go on up here and know that Jerry was going to be in big trouble, so I'd give them a few minutes, then walk back in and make up some story about how I wandered somewhere dangerous."

"Excellent," says Zip. "Now shut the bleep up and let's go."

Zip does hang from the garage roof to make the drop small, which I'm glad to see; save those calf muscles for some skate saves. Usually I jump, I did even when I was little, but I hang and drop too. ("We'll need some goals from you.") And, actually, this little act of caution is my final hockey-related thought. Once my feet hit the ground, I'm on my way to rock. I show Zip the way we climb up when we get back and he nods, and then we walk to the school.

As we come over this hill and can see the building, I say, "Aren't you always surprised when you see this place? I mean, when we went here it didn't seem so low and little."

He doesn't answer. Looking at his watch, he says, "We're a little late. I wanted to be the first ones here. But I bet Dooby beat us. That dude is *pumped*. You'd never think it. I mean, a *saxophone*."

"He's into it," I say. "The other day he spent ten

minutes explaining that it was called a 'bent soprano,' which is rare because sopranos are all straight now like brass clarinets but they sound *very* inferior and harsh and he's always been pretty pleased with his 'sweet tone.' Hearing Dooby say the word 'sweet' made me kind of sick to my stomach." We turn a corner and I can see some weird dull light coming out of the cafeteria windows. "What's—"

"Candles," Zip says. "Parker told me they just light a million candles all over the place. They had to get a special permit, it was a pain, he said, but the art-punks like a certain 'atmosphere.' They also just throw all of these huge pillows around to, like, lean or sit on as they discuss the great books they're going to write or something. The room looks like a real club." He laughs. "*We'll* give them some 'atmosphere.'"

I laugh too. "I got a few special atmosphere chords ready for them, at ten on the volume scale."

"Oh, and that's the other great thing," he says. "Parker set it up so you can plug in to, like, the P.A. or something, some big amp the school has, and he got a couple of mikes if any of the horns want to amplify their 'solos,' as he put it."

"So I get to play *really* loud?"

"You get to howl so they hear you on the moon, my man."

"All right." We get close. I see all the flickering light inside and through a window I catch a cool glint of the blue-sparkle finish on Zip's drums. "Hey, so he knows there are more of us, and that's okay with him?"

Zip smiles. "Anything's okay with him. The only thing he wanted to make sure of is that we don't suddenly start playing like, you know, a *band*, doing the right parts to the songs. I told him not to worry."

We walk in. Parker's over in a corner talking with some kids dressed in black clothes, holding drinks in plastic cups. He waves and keeps talking. The other people, including this girl sitting with her legs crossed on one of those cushions, who has hair that looks dark purple just on the top of her head, stare at us.

"Dig that stage," I say. I know I am grinning. My guitar is standing on this actual chrome guitar stand Parker must have swiped from the music room or someplace, all plugged in, looking like an honored instrument all ready for the great man. There is some kind of soft spotlight that lights up just the stage. It's the only thing on besides all those candles.

"Hello." I look to the right and see Shark step out of the shadows on the edge of the stage. He's holding this little black instrument, with the part that must be what he blows into looking like most of it must have broken off. He's dressed in a black suit with a white shirt and a black bowtie.

"Wow," I say.

He nods, sticks the skinny mouthpiece into his mouth, pulls it out. "I wear a Wings jersey to play hockey, I wear this to play music." He shrugs.

"You look the coolest," Zip says.

"Yeah," I say. "It worries me that you might be able to play some real music."

He frowns slightly. "Actually, although my studies have all been in the, er, euphonious classical mode, I have a private preference for the more experimental, even improvisational repertoire of certain contemporary composers. In other words," he says with a smile, "I'll probably sound as lunatic as the rest of you."

Next Dooby and Barry show up together. Barry is wearing what he always wears—a flannel shirt, old bluejeans with one knee out, scuffed-up sneakers, and a baseball cap pulled low. He just nods and goes off behind the stage to get out his trombone. Dooby, however, has gotten kind of dressed up. He's wearing these very baggy skate-punk shorts, kind of a sickly yellow background with black pistols on it, and a Russian hockey jersey that's black with red writing in that weird alphabet and red stars on the shoulders, and, as a nice touch, a loose bright orange safety patrol belt. No hat, but his shoes make up for it. They are these super-shiny plain black tie shoes with thick soles. No socks.

"How come they shine like that?" I ask him.

Dooby looks down. "You like 'em? My father bought them to go to a wedding a long time ago. It's called patent leather. They're a little big for me but not much, because he's such a little doot. And besides, the big look kind of fits, don't you think?"

"It all fits just fine," I say.

He goes to get his sax out. By this time, quite a

few more of our "audience" have arrived and spread themselves around the edge of the room. They are all wearing black clothes, they have all had something pierced—one guy has a silver ring through an eyebrow—and they all give us a good look before settling down to talk.

Just then Prince arrives. Dooby and Barry and Zip and I all kind of gape as he walks slow and dignified across the floor. He's wearing a really nice suit and shirt and tie, but the suit is hot pink and the shirt is royal blue and the tie is pale yellow with one black footprint in the middle. His shoes are the same color blue as his shirt and they're made of that same kind of extra-shiny leather as Dooby's. The suit fits him, but it's very baggy in some places and tight in others, and it moves really cool when he walks, so he just takes his time.

"Bandmates," he says with a nod as he gets to the stage.

"You look nice in pink, sweetheart," says Dooby.

Prince smiles but doesn't react otherwise. There's something serious about him tonight, but happy, too, and kind of private. He looks down at himself. "This suit belongs to my grandfather," he says.

"The guy who taught you to sing," I say.

"It's called a zoot suit." He's also wearing a big watch chain that swings to his knees and a very thin yellow leather belt. "It comes with a righteous hat with a big brim, but, I don't know, somehow I thought the hat was too much."

We all laugh. "Also, it didn't fit," he says.

Everybody gets set up. The only guy missing now is Billy, and frankly, I don't think anybody is inclined to wait for him. Billy *isn't* really one of the dudes, I guess, but mostly it's his father who gets in the way. I figure Billy would never really do anything like sneak out on the night before a game, or probably anytime, and also probably the night before games his father takes him through a two-hour review of the fine points of his play, using video footage from our games as well as his own incredible wisdom (he's always hollering at Billy to do this or that, and every time Billy comes off the ice he tells him at least three things he didn't do), and then makes him put on boxing gloves for three or four rounds of sparring and then makes him drink a steroid milkshake and then locks him in his room.

We're almost ready, and there's about thirty or forty people in black out there on the cushions, so I look at Parker until he looks at me and I raise my eyebrows. He checks his watch, then nods.

Just then Billy comes running in with his trumpet case. And—surprise!—he is not alone. One of our other spazzes, a kid we call Allround because he also plays two other travel sports he is actually *good* at (football and baseball), is with him, carrying a violin case. Allround lives next door to Billy, he's a pretty cool kid, just sucks at hockey. Behind them both is Shinny, with a cast on one hand and a tambourine in the other. He lives just up their street. They are all wearing their Wings road jerseys.

Billy arrives all breathless and wide-eyed, trying awkwardly to open his case and get out his horn. "Take your time, man," says Prince, nodding to Allround and punching Shinny on the shoulder.

Billy is panting. "Told my dad team meeting, ride with Shinny's father," he says. "Players only, work out problems, Cody called it."

"A team meeting until two A.M.? But it's cool," says Prince. "Calm down, get your ax, take your places." He turns to Allround, who has pulled out a violin and a bow and is standing beside Barry. "You been told how this music works?"

Allround nods. "I play mostly bluegrass," he says. "I'll fit right in."

"What's bluegrass?" I ask.

"The white equivalent of jazz," says Prince. "From places like the mountains of Tennessee or Kentucky or other white places. Kind of hillbilly."

"You just wait," says Allround, with a smile. "I'll get you moving those fancy blue feet of yours." He puts part of the violin under his chin and gets his bow ready.

"Shinny, you bang that thing when the spirit moves you," says Prince. Then he looks at me. "Ready?"

I nod.

He flicks on his microphone. "Ladies and gentlemen," he says and we all kind of look up, because his voice, sounding very good, is coming out of speakers somewhere, amplified. Faces above black sweaters turn our way in the candlelight. "Ladies and gentlemen, poets and painters, dancers and novelists. For your listening pleasure, may I present the orchestra that has the honor of playing for you tonight." He lifts one arm and sweeps it back at us. "We are called . . . No Bleeping Idea."

He snaps a finger behind his back and I wham a huge four-finger chord that clangs out of the speakers and sounds like a hundred dropped frying pans. It hangs there in the air for a second—I swear I see the candle flames all move—and then I hit it again and Zip pops his snare and I start to quick-pick my low string just as Dooby squawks into a long line of notes and Barry does a march thing. Billy, who actually has a great tone, tries to follow Dooby but can't, so he kind of joins Barry, playing jazzy little things between Barry's nice blocky *oomps*, and Zip moves to the cymbals and floor tom and I see but don't hear Shinny smack the tambourine with his cast. Prince has begun to kind of roll through this no-word *bum-de-bum-bum* thing down low, sounds excellent, and then above it all there are these two new squealy things playing fast bunches of *very* high notes and I guess it's Shark's oboe and Allround's violin, never heard an oboe before and it is *ugly*, but it fits, it fits. I find another chord with three fingers midway up the neck and start a kind of offbeat rhythm playing a little softer, and I realize now you can hear *everybody*, clear, and it adds up to *big sound*. Then Prince, off my chords, starts a song about how high the moon is, and it is complete. We are *playing*.

Used to be of course I was the loudest, when it was Zip and me or even us with Prince, and I guess I *could* be the loudest now too but I find a way of playing hard and staying just very loud enough and keeping it booming but making it so everyone else sounds good and strong too. Allround shocks the crap out of me, playing these jolly square dance tunes *perfect* but in pieces that fit in, right between Shark's clusters of notes like very long needles and Dooby's swooping and wailing. Billy and Barry really keep something almost regular going, but Barry will switch his pattern every now and then and Billy will fill the spaces with some fast notes one time, a couple of slow ones another, or a silence broken by one quick kind of *blat*. Zip is beneath it all, doing lots of rolls on the tom-toms and snare, double-beats on his bass drum, and just at the right moment smashing a cymbal. I still can't hear Shinny, but he can hear himself I guess, because he's practically headbanging back and in fact once he smacks the skin of the tambourine right into his forehead for a few beats.

Prince is out in front, stepping sharp and dancing in little dabs, crooning right from one song through a little *boopity-bop-yeah-yeah* into another, moving that suit in swirls, perfect on some inside beat he just knows, as if we were, like, some well-organized 1932 jazz band playing in time behind him. Prince has studied for this.

We just go and go and there is always somewhere to move to, some space opens up ahead and you just see how to get there and how to fill it, and someone slips in on your tail and somebody jumps ahead of you and you find yourself following. Then it splinters, and suddenly instead of being chased by Allround while you tail Dooby between Barry's lows and Shark's highs, you find yourself right in the middle, fanning out chords like wings, and there's Billy on one side burbling off the high notes in the chord and there's Allround on the other, suddenly playing long and low and loud off the bottom of the chord. It's the most complicated thing you've ever been caught in the middle of, and it's the simplest too.

It is completely simple. Because it just keeps going on, because everyone is working so hard, listening and thinking and hustling. I get to look around the most because my head is free, and I watch all these faces, most with their eyes closed, as they just go and give it all away, and I almost start to feel tears coming several times. And I think: I *like* these dudes. This is my *team*.

Out past Prince, on the floor, people are dancing. *Lots* of them. Some are in pairs, some are alone, some of the dancing looks like the usual boy–girl stuff but some is different. Two or three people dance by themselves and they seem to know what they're doing, with spins and these long leaps, slicing through the crowd, using the whole room, end to end. One group of about eight people must have been in some Broadway musical or something together, because they are locked into this snappy routine, matching each other step for step and slide for slide, laughing. Two girls and two guys are standing just off to the left of the stage, headbanging all together in a line.

I feel like we control them all, we move them all, they are just the music.

We never take a break, not even Prince, though at several points he just sings syllables, but very melodious, and several times he hums, and several times he floats in this long falsetto *ooooooooooooo* above it all, and once he whistles, for maybe five minutes, as if he were some instrument. He *is* an instrument, maybe the best, but we're all freaking *great*.

At some point too, I have no idea when, some more guys from the team seem to have showed up. Woodsie, tall and serious, wearing a black turtleneck that makes his blond hair look white and carrying an electric bass trailing a plug wire, squeezes between Dooby and Billy and carefully finds just enough space to lower the neck, and without ever moving anything but his hands begins to play this walking rhythm you don't hear but you feel in your feet. And right beside me Ernie shows up with the biggest horn I have ever seen except for a tuba, and he has to kind of get inside it and he sees me watching and smiles and nods and yells to me what kind of a horn it is but I can't hear, I just nod. The sound his horn makes is awesome—it's like we have just added a bear to the zoo.

We roar. More people dance. Some of them have their heads back and are singing, but you can't hear it. Probably somewhere someone is carrying on a serious conversation about literature, but from here it looks like these art-punks know how to boogie and have cut loose. After so long, I'm so used to all of the sounds, I'm listening so hard to everyone, that it takes me a couple of minutes to notice that Ernie's horn has stopped and he has been hollering in my ear. I twang one long chord and use my tremolo bar to make it hang and wave in the air, and then I can hear him.

"What?" I scream.

"I said, check out your dad dancing." He grins and points with his chin somewhere out on the floor.

"My dad?" I scream. "My father? He's here?"

Ernie nods big nods and hollers something else. I wave another chord and lean closer.

"How do you think we got here?" he shrieks.

"Who? How?"

"Me and Woodsie," he hollers. "He brought us."

I feel like I'm skating and about to fall down. "My dad? He picked you up and brought you here?"

Ernie nods and rolls his eyes like, "Finally you

get it." Then he starts to play again. Playing another chord automatically, I look out past Prince, past the headbangers, past a bunch of people in motion, and then I see him, way in the back, with his light gray hair and his nylon Wings parka with *Coach* stitched in script over his heart, laughing and talking as he sort of dances with this skinny girl in tight black clothes who has orange hair and a nose ring. She's laughing and answering him and dancing too. He's snapping his fingers. He doesn't look ridiculous though. He looks happy, like everybody else.

While I watch him he looks up and catches my eye. His expression of pure happiness doesn't change. He nods at me, nods toward the whole band, makes a circle with his arms. He's grinning like he will break. The girl he's dancing with thinks he's doing some dance move, so she makes a circle with her arms too, and he sees this and laughs and resumes dancing with her with his full attention.

And I go back to my music. It's still there even though my father is too, it's moving right along, all of us hustling together, and he's dancing to it. All of a sudden I find some interesting place between a snare roll of Zip's that seems almost to be playing a tune and a long melody Allround keeps playing, and I get a chord that fits right in there and strum it in a different way, with the heel of my hand almost against the strings, and it sounds just right, a little muffled and drummy, a little soft-twangy in a way that could be called hillbilly, and in fact Allround looks over his violin at me and smiles and nods like *we know*. And so it keeps going, one thing after another, until I think we are going to play all night.

We probably would, but I see the back door open and a security guard comes in and talks to my dad, and my dad nods, and asks a couple of people something, and then somebody goes and gets Parker and the security guy talks to him and Parker nods and grabs his head like "I had no idea!" and nods and they nod and then he works his way through the crowd up to the front of the stage in front of Prince. Prince finishes a verse, holds his mike against his chest and leans over, bobbing all the while. Parker hollers something in his ear. Prince straightens up and nods, still bobbing, and turns around and looks at me. He holds up two fingers. I nod. He looks at each guy playing and

holds them up, singing again now, until it's one finger, and he's still singing but he makes a circle over
his head with his hand. One time—and I crash a
huge chord as loud as I can—two times—I crash
another—and then a third time and I crash it and
strum, handling the pick so the strums get softer
and softer fast and everyone has a chance to wind
up what he's doing and spin down and taper out,
and soon it's just Zip tapping his snare and hi-hat
and me strumming very soft now, and it's nice, we
keep it going for one minute more, and then Prince,
holding his mouth right against the microphone,
says in this low soft voice that sounds like it is
coming from inside your head, "Good night, ladies
and gentlemen, poets and painters. It has been our
pleasure to give you . . . No Bleeping Idea!" and I hit
one last chord and Zip snaps a rimshot and all of
a sudden it's over, the music is over, and we are
all staring at each other. In a minute we start grinning and slapping hands quietly, like now our job
is silence, but there is still noise and it is the art-
punks, cheering and screaming and clapping. They
keep it up for minutes, then the security guy comes
back in and flicks the lights on and off and the

cheering winds down and then, then, it is really over.

I glance around and everyone is looking half stunned and half happiest-he's-ever-been. Prince is hugging a trim old dude with white hair who is exactly his size and is clapping him on the back and I guess it's his grandfather, Prince must have invited him, he must have been somewhere listening. Then Billy's dad is there and he's smiling and clapping at Billy, who looks terrified but then, when his dad keeps clapping, lets his happiness come back.

Parker is onstage shaking each player's hand, and when he gets to me he says, "I've told everyone to just put it in the case and leave, while it's still nice and candlelit and all. I apologize, but I let things go, and it's almost three o'clock, so in a minute we have to turn up the lights and clean up. I'm going to take Zip's drums down and keep them in the van until he calls me tomorrow. So, unplug, and thank you, Cody, it was great beyond belief, find your case, get your buddies together, and all of you should meet your father outside as fast as possible. Oh, and here, there's this." He hands me an envelope.

We do what he says, and as we leave we're walking through the art-punks who are leaving too, and as they pat us on the back and the head and say nice things and give little cheers, one voice says, "These are really *kids*!" and another says, "Genuine punks. We're just posers." Then we're all suddenly outside, and I look around and see my dad off a ways, on the edge of the parking lot, leaning up against his truck with his legs crossed, waving one arm for us to come. I kind of don't want to be the first to get there so I hang back a little, and then Zip is with me and we walk behind Dooby and Billy and Barry, who are strolling over like there was absolutely nothing wrong about being discovered by your hockey coach playing music at three in the morning before a game at six. My dad doesn't look at me exactly, he just checks that everybody is there, and then he says, "Okay, listen up," and everybody gets quiet.

He looks at us for a few seconds, a *long* few seconds. Everybody suddenly kind of seems to remember where we are and what time it is, and it gets *real* quiet. But just before the happy mood can float down, my dad says, "I have two questions."

"Let's hear them," says Prince.

"Okay," says my dad. He holds up a finger, smiling. "One: Can anyone tell me—what kind of music was that?"

We laugh, and Prince says, "We *told* you exactly what kind it was." He turns to us. "We told them all. We told them exactly what they got tonight, didn't we, guys? So let's tell Coach now, all together, because apparently he wasn't listening, so"—He lifts his arm—"all together, uh-one, uh-two, uh-three—"

"*No bleeping idea!*" we all holler at my dad. He frowns, cups his hand behind an ear, and leans toward us, so we shout it again, as loud as we can, "*No bleeping idea!*"

"Thank you!" he says. "Now I know what I've been listening to. Precisely."

"What's your second question?" Prince asks.

"Ah," says my dad, nodding. "That's right. Second question. Very important." He holds up two fingers. "My second question has to do with my truck."

He turns and looks it up and down, and all of us

kind of go "Wha?" and look at it too. Then he turns back to us. "The question about my truck is this: Can we fit all of you, and your instruments, most of which are way smaller than hockey bags, all into my truck so we can drive back to our house where, just about now"—he looks at his watch again— "Cody's mother is putting on the table a breakfast of scrambled eggs with cheese and bacon and oatmeal and fresh-baked cinnamon rolls and coffee? That," he says, "is my second question."

"And the answer," says Prince, turning to us and holding his arm up again, "is that until we try it we have—"

"*No bleeping idea.*"

So we try it, and we all fit, and although I didn't say so, I knew we would. The record for this truck is the same number of kids, but with hockey bags, and they were Peewees, who are bigger. My dad was right. A Squirt with a violin case is a lot smaller than a Peewee with a hockey bag.

Breakfast is great. It turns out to be almost the same feeling as when we were playing, except that instead of giving something out, we are putting something in. We eat and eat, jabbering about the gig, and my dad makes us each finish with a full cup of black coffee. Then we get a little quiet, and he looks at us, smiling, and looks at his watch, and says, "Well—are you ready?"

"*Ready!*" we holler.

"And what *else* are you?"

"No bleeping idea!" says Billy, but everyone else knows what my dad means and is quiet, until Prince, the voice, says, "Coach, we are actually a hockey team."

My dad nods. "That's what I think, too. You are certainly a team of some sort. So let's go get in the hockey coach's truck, and go to the hockey rink, and put on our hockey skates, and pick up our hockey instruments, and see if we can just move this thing right out onto the ice and keep on playin'."

We jump up with a whoop and go.

# *eleven*

ctually, when we get to the rink it's kind of late. Coach asked Billy's dad to go and collect every kid's bag and so our stuff is laid out and waiting in the locker room really nice, and when the first kid comes in and sees it, I think it's Allround, he starts to thank Billy's dad but Billy's dad raises his hand and says, "You're welcome, you're welcome, just get your young tails dressed and on the ice," and so everyone jumps into his stuff in a hurry. Coach comes in and sets up the lines and gives the shifts and nobody has any time to talk or anything. We're quick and concentrated and in a hurry, and then we're running out and hopping onto the ice and Bowie is already there, they've already warmed up, and now they're doing the usual pass-and-shoot drill with pucks. Our side of the ice is shiny and blank except for Boot and a spaz named Joe, who we couldn't figure out a nickname for because he's got nothing to mock except his hockey skills and so far he hasn't done anything funny. These two are skating around kind of lazy and Boot says nothing but studies us hard and we can't explain, just can't. We wheel around the ice a few times, getting the feel as fast as we can, then the buzzer sounds and we have to race to the bench and shuffle in and out and then the first line of Prince at center and me and Boot with Barry and Dooby on D just gets lined up and the ref drops the puck. Time to play.

From the start, we are all *over* them. In their big black uniforms the Bowie goons look like soda machines on wheels or something, but we are *music team*, we flow, man, we go to strange places together and know we are surrounded and backed up, and a pass to one of our guys feels like leading his violin or sax into a cool place to do some damage, and before you know it, we score. Nobody knows who got the goal, we're all just buzzing, we feel like we all shot it, and the ref gives it to Allround. Off the second face-off Bowie makes a rush but it seems clumsy and I laugh, no reason, it's just this feeling that these guys don't *get* it—

how could they? Then Prince says, "Take a solo, baby," and drops me the puck coming out of the zone off a blocked shot by Barry and I take off, past two guys, with a stutter step like double-picking a string, and in their zone I get both D coming at me sideways at a stupid angle and I crash a chord here with a sharp skeet stop, hear my skates bite and crunch like *chong* on all six strings, and I scramble back as the D fly by helpless. I close in on the goalie and look him in the eye and shoot before he expects me to, high over the far shoulder into the exact geometrical corner where net meets posts *cha!* and I laugh, and circle back, and all the guys are laughing too. I whip my stick up like my guitar and wham my right arm. Coach calls our shift off.

"Don't hotdog, Cody," he says. "They're asleep and we don't want to wake 'em up yet."

"Just playing my ax," I say.

The next shift has it too. You can see they *feel* each other out there, it's like they all of a sudden have Woodsie's strange way of knowing where everyone is on the ice but it's more, hard to explain, but there's something to it of liking your guys, being with them and doing something reckless and fast, and there's something, maybe the biggest part, about feeling you can count on people. I'll tell you, I've been on some great teams with almost too much talent, but for parts of every season, even every game, I have felt like I was all alone out there. I think everybody goes through this. But it's history now with *these* guys. Our forwards are buzzing again, circling and keeping the puck and playing, making a sudden blind pass across the whole ice that would seem amazing or ridiculous if you didn't feel the possibility of it open up yourself. The third shift, which includes Shark and Joe, starts to play but loses the puck, and our spazzes get caught up ice and the big black soda machines bear down on Zip, three of them, with only Woodsie back. They play it perfectly, one pass between the wingers and then a back pass to the trailer, who lets go an outrageous slapper from the high slot and Zip catches it from his knees, leaning the other way. He tosses the puck at the kid who shot it and the ref gives Zip a warning. Big deal. Zip laughs.

It's like it's unfair, it's like we're playing another game out there, we're all grinning, and every time you look at a guy you think of him last night, face sweaty, eyes closed, pushing his horn someplace, working hard, and then you see him hipcheck a bigger kid and recover the puck and tap it to a teammate and you know he's still just working hard, it's all the same, we've got it now.

Unfortunately we also have spazzes and they give up too many rushes and Zip can't stop one where he flops, fooled by a deke shot before a late pass, and a Bowie kid tips it into the open net and after a while the period ends, 2–1 us.

When we gather at the bench we're not grinning anymore, we're not playing half music, half hockey, we're maybe getting a little tired, but there's still the feeling, and we glance around, maybe give a quick nod, and we know it. Coach does too. He says, "You got it. Hang onto it. You're going to get pretty tired, so save something. Get one more and I bet we have 'em. They're not sure they're on the same ice as you."

We go out and play and it *is* a little slower, maybe the concentration slips here and there, but we are still flowing around those guys like a river around rocks. The forwards play better defensively because you can do that when you're tired, except Boot, who doesn't play any defense, and is not tired anyway, and scores a very pretty goal cutting across the slot with a defenseman on his back reaching his stick around but can't quite get at the puck, which Boot backhands soft but in just the right spot and then casually throws the defenseman backwards onto his butt. A couple of Bowie bad guys skate up to Boot and Barry skates up to them and Woodsie cuts in, but they all hear Coach's voice: "*No*. Save it," and they skate away.

Bowie's coach calls a timeout and I think he tells them we're tired because they start to skate harder and pass longer and force us to cover more ice. Then they get one on a slapshot from the point while two of their forwards and both of our D screen Zip. He never sees it, but he's furious anyway and sticks the puck from the net and slings it high over the glass, and the ref gives him a penalty. It's almost the end of the period. On their power play we're a step behind the play, and all of a sudden the open guy is standing at the left post with the puck and he buries it. Absolutely not Zip's fault, except it *was* his penalty, but all of a sudden we are tied.

We all skate to the bench together and Coach looks us over. "You're beat," he says. "I just want to know one thing. Do you still have it, somewhere beneath the fatigue? Can you find it and count on it and make it play? Like last night? Like the first period? You are the same people who did all that. You're the team that put all that together, as long ago as it seems."

"How do we play it?" Prince asks. He sounds fine, but quiet.

Coach looks around. "You have lost almost every game bad. You probably won't lose any more that bad. This can be a kind of transition." He pauses. "How would a tie feel?"

Everybody thinks. "I'll take a tie," says Dooby. "And I hate ties."

"Zip?" Coach asks.

"I'll keep it out of the goal. Whether you guys score is up to you. If we tie, I'll feel fine. If we win, I won't be jumping around drinking champagne anyway."

"Cody," he says finally. "What do you think?"

"I think we can play together, but, like, right now maybe in just one way," I say. "Right now I think we can stay tight by playing coordinated defense and driving them crazy by being all over them. And who knows? They may get careless and we get a break and win. But I say let's just concentrate on not even letting them get a shot. Doing it together for a tie—for our first freaking even *tie* of the season, don't forget, our first *point*—is still doing it together. I think that's all we have left."

Coach nods. "Anybody else? Anybody disagree with your captain's plan?"

We all look at each other and we're still hard and tough and happy, and we know even though we have just agreed to go for a wimpy-sounding tie that it's okay, we're all right like this.

Boot raises his glove. Coach nods. "The Boot would just like to say ties suck." He pauses. "But the Boot—the Boot will play a little D, because the Boot is a complete player." Everybody laughs, but Boot doesn't. He holds up his glove again. "And the Boot belongs to this team," he says quietly, his chin held high.

Bowie plays right into our hands. They have decided to be aggressive and reckless and ignore the fact that they are covered, so time and time again we intercept and flip it out of the zone and they skate back in and press something that won't work and we cut it off and slide the puck down ice and they chase it and come storming back. Practically the whole third period is played in our end, but we are grim and every five-guy shift plays perfectly coordinated, and by the time there is a minute left they have not gotten a single shot on goal. Then somebody gets a slippery little backhander through some traffic and it hits a skate and gets past Zip, but good old Dooby, keeping his head, skips behind Zip and skates it out of the crease and fires it to me and I look up and both defensemen have hustled back and I think, *You know? We've already done it to you guys,* and I flip it to a corner instead of trying to be the hero. They get it back in the zone and just start firing slapshots from everywhere, but not one of them even gets through to Zip and the buzzer sounds and we got the tie, we got an actual point, and Bowie is humiliated, and suddenly we are happy again and we mob Zip and everybody flops over into a pile.

Zip usually starts screaming at this point and

cussing bad, but now he does the strangest thing. He just says, *"Thump. Thump. Thump thump thump. Smash, tap tap, boom boom."* And I get it: He's playing the drums, there on the bottom of the pileup. I pitch in by yelling *"Chang chang whong"* as loud as I can but it isn't too loud, but Barry feels it and starts saying *"Oompah wha wha oomp,"* and Dooby and Billy start singing lines, and Allround and Shark do their whines and finally Prince, on top, does some *"Shooby-dooby-dooby-baby"* and sings one verse of one song, I don't remember anything it was about, while we all yammer beneath him and then, when he finishes, we are all quiet, and are all together, for a long long time.

Here's a sneak peek at the next book in the

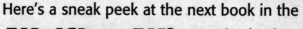 ice hockey

series by Bruce Brooks

available from HarperCollins

The Columbia left wing who is supposed to be checking the Boot glances over his shoulder as he skates into the neutral zone to chase Prince carrying the puck. Sure enough, as the wing thought, the slow old Boot is trudging along, head down, a few steps behind, losing ice with each stride. Looks like he *might* make it to the blue line after the play has been completed and they have to turn around to come the other way, and then he'll have to stop, turn, and do it all over . . .

The Columbia left wing decides he can cheat a little on his coverage—he doesn't like the way that little kid Cody is trailing Prince into the zone with some stop-and-go moves that are giving fits to his teammate, the Columbia center. Sure enough, as the wing watches, Cody turns the center the wrong way and slips around him clean to the other side, now trailing Prince without any check.

In half a second the left wing decides to abandon his slow-Boot responsibility back there; he darts to catch up with Cody and slash at his stick from behind. Cody veers hard left as Prince speeds up on his way down the high slot, stickhandling, hypnotizing the defenseman skating backwards in front of him, drawing the dude's eyes down at the puck, where the left wing knows he shouldn't be looking.

Prince skeets almost to a stop and circles tightly to make what he obviously thought would be an easy flip pass to Cody cutting in behind the D from the left circle. But the dutiful Columbia wing who left old Boot in his ice chips has kept after Codes and now manages just to hook his right glove enough to spin him a tiny bit upright and sideways as he cuts to the net. Cody wobbles slightly, but it ought to be enough to make him miss that pass, which is no doubt zipping right now to intersect his unimpeded dash at the net. *Yes!* thinks the Columbia wing. *I broke up the play!*

The only thing is, Prince, although he is looking right at Cody, does something else entirely. And he seems to have been planning on it all along: He snaps a low blind backhand pass the *other* way, past the defenseman to the *right*. Is he nuts? There can't be anybody over *there* to get the puck! It will go to the corner and the Columbia D will pick it up and skate it out of the zone. The left wing, still hooking Cody's glove, looks up—as does Cody, now coasting nice and slow—to watch this happen.

But instead of Nobody over on that side, there, instead of harmless blank ice, there is Someone, someone planted at the far post with his skates spread and his stick drawn back eight inches, ready to one-time that pass into a gaping net. It is, glory be, the old Boot. Just as the Columbia wing is thinking "How did *he* get here?" Boot's stick—only the stick, none of the rest of that cloddish body— moves in a blur through those eight inches and the next thing you know, the puck is bulging the old twine behind the sprawling goalie like a cannonball.

The Columbia wing lets his stick blade droop to the ice. Cody and Prince are rubbing the scorer's helmet as he turns, without even raising his arms, and trudges back to his bench. "Hey, nice freakin' coverage," the Columbia goalie screams at his wing.

"Your little sister could check that dude." The wing ignores him, staring at the far post, where the Boot was waiting for that perfect blind backhand pass from Prince. But—how?—the guy was way back there and—

Well, it's a sad, common tale. But the fact is, the Boot leaves a lot of broken hearts on the ice. . . .

The Boot's Lesson One in goal Scoring: Disappear. Lesson Two: Show up at the last possible moment, just as the puck arrives. Lesson Three: Do the simple thing and put it in the rope.

Probably the hardest part is learning how to disappear. Maybe it's even one of those things you can't learn; maybe it's just a gift. If so, the Boot has always been blessed with it. The Boot was born to disappear.